THE
GREAT GAME

(McPhee – a Football Tale)

The Great Game

(McPhee – a Football Tale)

Sydney Horler

www.1889books.co.uk

ISBN: 978-1-915045-23-2

INTRODUCTION

This novel was first published in 1923 under the name *McPhee – a football story*. It is a pretty rubbish title by today's standards and is perhaps why when it was later re-published they changed the title to *The Great Game*. Hedging my bets, I decided to stick with the latter, and use McPhee in the subtitle. It is a very interesting novel in many respects. Not only is it an easy read, full of dry wit in the style of Wodehouse, but it is a must-read for any fan of the history of the game. It was Horler's third football novel, after *Goal!* and *The Legend of the League* (also republished by 1889 Books).

In my opinion it is the most rounded of his football novels, with a sound plot and a character in Angus McPhee who has some depth, and a backstory that gives us insight into the character's actions. It doesn't go as far as being able to be described as a character-driven novel and we don't get a lot of what his emotions and feelings are but we can believe in him as a human being. The plot is also quite strong and Horler does write really well about the game and its importance. To illustrate both these points, take this extract where McPhee is reflecting on the possibility of the team he is the trainer for no longer existing:

> In the course of time, the trainer took himself out to the long bench by the white railings below the grand-stand, which was his seat of office when a match was on, and once again gazed at the scene which had become so familiar – so dearly familiar – to him.
>
> He felt something gripping him. All his hopes were centred on that patch of churned turf, with the white goal-posts standing sentinel at either end. It was here he had laboured, putting not only all his physical but his mental strength into the job. If he were banished now from that open-air workshop of his, it would be infinitely harder than it had been a few weeks back. Then he had only *intended* to do – now he had actually *done* it – not half, nor yet a quarter of what he hoped, but still something, a great deal even, considering the time.

At the beginning of the 1920s Horler was looking around for an idea of something to write about to capture the popular imagination "as a regular source of fiction material." It was a game at Craven Cottage between Fulham and Bristol City who he followed as a schoolboy that gave him the idea. He wrote: "I hadn't seen a professional football match since my school days but Lady Luck now led me to the ground of a professional football club once again. Directly I saw the scarlet jerseys of the team whose fortunes I had so passionately followed as a youngster something like 20 years slipped away from my shoulders and I became a schoolboy again. Then came the inspiration: no-one, apart from boys' comic writers, had ever turned England's greatest national sport, into fiction. So I resolved to have a shot at it myself…"

Horler started out on his pioneering idea of writing a football novel full of enthusiasm. He wrote in his 1922:

> "Some say that professional football is a very dull subject about which to write. But that is all a point of view; the national sport of any country must have a wonderful human interest and if there was not something inspiriting and stimulating about Big Football the great sporting public would not throng in their countless thousands to the matches every Saturday."

That sounds logical, but his enthusiasm soon cooled, despite one of his novels *The Ball of Fortune* being turned into a silent movie. He turned his attention instead to the thrillers for which he is best known. By 1933 he wrote this in his autobiography:

> "I have proved from experience that the people who go
> in their millions to football matches are not willing to spend
> money on buying books dealing with their favourite sport."

The problem was, and still is, the snobbery of the middle-class literary elite: who have always had a firm stranglehold over the publishing industry: both from a writing perspective and from the decision-making about what will sell. It is true that a love for football doesn't translate into a love of reading a book that has a football theme – other than, often tedious, ghostwritten autobiographies for some reason. There was of course a dalliance with Fever Pitch – it certainly caught a mood in the early 90s and tickled a London literary scene that had newly discovered football, finding it briefly trendy in the wake of Gazza's Italia 90 tears. But can it even be described as fiction. Isn't it more a self-indulgent whinge than a story? Does anyone doubt that it would have disappeared without trace if it had been written about Notts County, Bury FC or Crewe Alexandra and not the metropolitan elite of Arsenal? No one should be surprised – publishing is after all a branch of the fashion industry. What sells is not necessarily good, but trendy and marketable to the early thirties female on the Northern Line or the working from home hipster to read over breakfast at that trendy little café over a £9 bowl of porridge and a £4 turmeric latte. They will read a Hardy classic with a farming theme even if they know nothing about farming, but heaven forefend they would go near a classic like *The Hollow Ball* or *The Thistle and the Grail*, because football is for oiks. You can read a book about a person with any other job in the world and enjoy it for the story and the literature, but if the main character is into football or a footballer – then if must be worthless. *The Blinder* is probably Barry Hines finest novel, but, good though it is, it is *A Kestrel for a Knave* that everyone bangs on about – in fact it is usually the film *Kes* that people remember, and they've not even the book.

It is often claimed that baseball and American football have inspired great novels, so why can't Association football produce a great novel? (In fact Horler drew inspiration from Charles Evan Loan who, in the early 1900s, created popular fiction based around baseball.) However, this claim is nothing than a lazy myth. As well as those mentioned, I could also cite *Papeles en el Viento* by Eduardo Sacheri, *Abide With Me* by Ian Ayris, and *Dans La Foule* by Laurent Mauvignier. All of these are as good as, and in my opinion, better than the raved about American baseball novels *The Natural* and *Shoeless Joe*. And don't even get me started on *American Pastoral*. *The Ghosts of Inchmery Road* and *The Lives of Stanley B* by Mat Guy are also superb novels that haven't received the recognition they deserve.

Of course I don't claim that Horler is up there with the best football novels, but the very fact he was a pioneer makes him worth reading. To the modern reader some of his work could be regarded as full of footballing clichés, but it has to be remembered that he was writing only 30 years after the game really took off and so cannot be regarded that way. Shakespeare's works are full of (what are now) clichés – but they were original or fresh ways of thinking back then (as with all clichés – the person who first said "kettle calling pot black" probably had their mates saying: "ooh, that's clever, I'll pinch that.")

The Great Game/McPhee draws on the growing folklore surrounding what was already by then a firmly embedded national obsession. For example, there are references to the legendary occasion when Sheffield United's Harry Thickett supposedly played on despite having several broken ribs by dint of getting his chest heavily bandaged up, and there are references to some of the early legends in the game such as John Doig and L.R. Roose

Another fascinating aspect is McPhee's approach to coaching, which at the time would have read as being very modern: a scientific approach and getting the players to work as a unit – as a team better than the sum of their parts – something that even some modern day managers could learn from.

I have written in the Introduction to Stanley Horler's *On the Ball!* about how problematic some of his writing and views are. *McPhee* is less problematic than some of his other works, though there are some offensive descriptions of people based on their size. Horler was an admirer of the classical male physique and for someone who writes derisively elsewhere about "foppishly-dressed individuals" and "weaklings," the almost homo-eroticism of his admiration for his heroes could be the subject of analysis!

Angus McPhee (as with Goal!) could be regarded as full of footballing clichés, but being published in 1923 and 1920 respectively, they long-preceded all the Roy of the Rovers follow-ons. Although there was already an established tradition of short fiction in comics such as Boys' Own Paper, he certainly seems to have been the first person to turn this kind of writing into long-form fiction.

Sydney Horler was born in Leytonstone in Essex in July 1888. He was educated in Bristol at Redcliffe Boys School, then at a boarding school: Colston's (yes, him – of Bristol statue in the dock fame). After a brief foray into teaching he became a newspaper reporter at the *Western Daily Press* in Bristol in 1905, ending up in Fleet Street working on the *Daily Mail* and in a government propaganda department towards the end of the First World War. After the war he went to work for publisher George Newnes, a publisher of a lot of mass market and serialised fiction at the time. He died in a Bournemouth nursing home in October 1954 at the age of 66.

– Steven Kay 2024

CHAPTER I

THE DOWNSIDE DIRECTORS RECEIVE A SHOCK

Sadness hung about him like a foggy halo. It pervaded and permeated the man, seeming to exude from his clothes and mingle with the rain that dripped from the almost unbelievable hat he carried his hand. He had come out of the black night like a visitant from another world.

'My name, gentlemen,' he said in an accent strongly Scottish, 'is McPhee – Angus McPhee.'

To the directors of the Downside F.C. it seemed an admirable name for such a man. They were too surprised to say anything. They had advertised for a trainer for their professional football team, and this man had presented himself as an applicant. Anyone less like a trainer than the man standing before them, it would have been impossible to conceive. He might have been a vegetarian undertaker, or an impecunious professor of Scottish divinity, they decided; but he certainly was not a football trainer.

'It doesn't interest us what your name is,' said the chairman, Benjamin Fortey, head of a firm of local hauliers. 'We're looking for a football trainer, not a Baptist minister, mister. You've come to the wrong shop – the chapel's on the other side of the road!' He sniggered as he finished.

The sad-looking stranger held up one of his black-gloved hands, and there was something in the gesture which commanded attention, almost respect.

'Gentlemen,' he said; 'I have no come to the wrong place. Ye advertised for a football trainer; weel, I'm here!'

'What the – ?' the amazed and almost indignant chairman started to splutter, but the sight of that uplifted black-gloved hand seemed to hypnotise him. He lapsed into his seat and smouldering silence.

'Ye'll be wantin' to know something aboot me before ye gi'e me the job,' the stranger continued. 'My name, as I ha'e already telt you, is McPhee – Angus McPhee. I am forty years of age, and sound in wind and limb, with the exception of a wee limp in the left leg. My pairsonal appearance maybe will make ye laugh: weel, it has made ither folk laugh; but that's no my fault. After I was wounded in the War, I trained and coached the regimental football team which won the Brigade Championship, and after that the shield for the best regimental team in the B.E.F. I've got the highest grade certeeficates for massage and pheeysical culture.

'These are my qualifications. Ye'll do well to gi'e me the job.'

He glanced from one to the other of the directors of the Downside Football Club, who stared back at him in astonishment.' I'll ha'e ye onderstand that football is juist wife, child and releegion to me. That is why I shall ha'e to make a success of the job.

'Then, before anyone could find time to interrupt his steady flow of oratory, he was off once more, speaking sonorously and earnestly, and giving emphasis to his words by wavings of his black woollen gloves. He had the missionary gestures as well as the missionary spirit.

'You'll no be denyin' me that the game your team played on Saturday last was tairrible. It wasna' football at all. It might have been wrestling or anything else, but it was no football. All football at the present time is bad – but yours, gentlemen, is awful!'

To the Downside directors McPhee's scathing words were like an accusing conscience. If there was one team in the four countries of Great Britain and Ireland which was universally acknowledged by press and public alike to be playing deplorably bad football at that time, it was Downside. They had scored exactly three goals in twelve matches (and given away no fewer than thirty-three). They were at the bottom of the Second Division table, and looked likely to remain there.

'M'm!' mumbled the chairman, looking as though he wanted to bite someone – 'Well, get on!'

The stranger placed his degraded hat on the table, squared his shoulders, and like the Ancient Mariner, held them with his glittering eye. The only sound heard was the heavy breathing of Mr. Samuel Spurgeon, the eighteen-stone occupant of the vice-chair, who was asthmatic, and ought not to have been out in the night air.

'When I left the sairvice, I made up my mind to be a football trainer and coach. But' – and fire flashed from the eyes – 'they all laugh like the domned fools they are. Naebody would ha'e me. You're the last team I've approached, – but you're the worst. I put you at the bottom of my list.'

'Er!' grunted the chairman.

'You'll no take offence I hope – there's no man worth his salt that's afraid of the truth,' quickly responded McPhee, 'and I'm no complainin' – I shall ha'e a better chance with a football team like yours.'

Mr. Fortey felt it was up to him, as chairman, to get rid of this lunatic as quickly as possible – quietly, if feasible; with the aid of the police, if necessary.

'Yes, yes, Mr. – I forget your name for the moment; McPhee, is it ? – well, Mr. McPhee! Now we have wasted a good deal of time listening to what you have so kindly told us, and I'm sure you won't object if I say that it's getting late, and my friends and myself have a good many things to attend to. You quite understand – eh? What's the matter with you?'

To the amazement of all in the room, Mr. Angus McPhee, instead of accepting the very forcible hint that his presence was superfluous, took off his dripping overcoat and also removed his black woollen gloves. If signs and portents went for anything, he intended staying.

'Onderstand?' he said equably. 'Aye, mon, I onderstand: I've haird those words before, and I'm no likely to forget them. But don't be in a hurry to push me off. It is not as if you had a guid team thet I could spoil. Your side is as bad as it could be – deeplorable. In front of goal it's like a poleetical meeting. I'll show ye somethin' the noo.'

Before anyone could stop him, Angus McPhee had picked up a football which was lying in a corner of the room. He let it fall from his hands, and tapped it with his boot as it dropped. Immediately the ball seemed to be endowed with life; it ran up the long lean shank of McPhee, and, upon reaching the knee, it was jerked upwards and came to rest on the sandy head of the demonstrator, where it settled itself as comfortably as though that was its natural home.

'Pity I havena' more space at my deesposal,' commented McPhee, sliding the ball back into the corner from whence he had taken it, 'for then I could show ye better the power I've got over a football. That power, gentlemen, I can pass on to your players. Ye canna deny that scarcely a single yin o' them kens how to control a football.' He fairly hurled the charge at them.

The Downside directors were obviously impressed. They sat supinely in their chairs, and allowed the man still to babble on.

'It's no so much the money I'm thinking abooyt –'

'Don't you want to be paid?' cried Spurgeon stentoriously from the bottom of the table. Anyone who would work for nothing was an angel of light in Mr. Spurgeon's eyes; and at the same time a damned fool.

'Paid? Aye, but money isna' the first consideeration, ye understand. Until I can show you what I can do with the men I'll take small pay – say four poond a week.' He paused and then launched into another impassioned period: 'Dinna ye ken that football is an art, a science, and must be lairned properly.'

'What about a month's trial?' snapped the chairman, in the tone of a man giving away his last bottle of whisky. 'Only a month mind,' he added.

'Sir,' was the prompt reply, 'your terms are accepted. Gi'e me a month, and if at the end of that time your team doesna' win matches instead of losing them, I'll resign.'

'You'll have to!' flung back the chairman; 'and now for the Lord's sake stop talking, and let's have a look at those certificates you said you had on you.'

If Mr. Fortey imagined that the talkative and amazing stranger who had drifted into the meeting out of the night was to be caught in this simple manner, he was disillusioned. Without the slightest hesitation, Angus McPhee pulled a number of papers out from his pocket and passed them over.

'If you'd wait outside for a few minutes, we will give the matter consideration,' said the chairman, after he had satisfied himself that the various certificates were in order, and apparently genuine.

Inclining his head gravely, McPhee retired, looking longingly at the football with which he had demonstrated his "ball control" as though he would have liked to take it with him.

'Well?' demanded Mr. Fortey challengingly, directly the door was closed. 'Those things are all right,' he added, tapping the papers in front of him.

'Is *he* all right?' demanded a director; sitting half-way down the table on his right.

'He's barmy, if you ask *me*! I never heard talk so much in my life!'

Mr. Spurgeon shifted his gargantuan bulk.

'Try him, Ben!' he wheezed; 'he's cheap anyway; and seeing that sane people can't prevent this Club from going straight to the bone-yard, p'raps a loony can! Try him, Ben.'

'What do you say, gentlemen?' asked the chairman; 'As Sam says, he's cheap — *and he's the only one who has answered the advertisement.*'

Shaken by terrific storms as they had been during this year of office, the other directors not the strength to resist the lead thus given them by the Chair, and supported so substantially by the Vice-Chair.

As the recalled and gratified McPhee was bowing his acknowledgments for his month's trial as trainer and coach of the discredited Downside F.C, a director was heard whispering to his neighbour: 'What will Ovens say.'

CHAPTER II

THE CLUB WITH A PAST

The Downside Football Club, over which Providence and his own peculiar and persuasive methods, had placed Angus McPhee, was a club with a past. It had seen better days, but of late years it had been an easy mark for the misguided efforts of a thoroughly incompetent Board of Directors. There was also Mr. Horace Ovens – but the moment for Mr. Ovens is not yet.

The time had been when Downside had flaunted its red and white favours amongst the elect of the First Division. Then it had been a team worthy of the town. Those were the days when to play for Downside was a joy and pride to some of the finest football craftsmen in the land. Who will ever forget the mazy, bewildering runs down the left wing by little Bobby Denton, that wonderful box o' tricks; the trenchant raids and cannon-ball shots of Big Bill Bradley, the centre-forward; the brainy, constructive half-back work of Dick Dean, Albert Knott, and "Simple Simon" Geekie?

That same team furnished one full back for an English International team, and another defender for Wales. Behind these two had stood, guarding the goal like a football Horatius, Jamie Dempter! What a team!

Football like Life, has its ups and downs. The wise directorate will prepare for the evil days; it will make its plans and be prepared for the inevitable slump. After losing its place in the First Division – six years previously – the directors did little more than publicly bewail their lot. Luck was against them, they said.

Luck – or what they designated luck – continued to be against them. Like the unwise virgins, they had no oil in their lamps – and precious little wick either. Also they continued to pay Mr. Horace Ovens his salary. Modern football is a business – where competition is the very breath of life, but the Downside officials resolutely refused to compete. Their only chance was to spend money in obtaining fresh players, yet they kept the cheque-book locked up in the office safe.

But that was not the chief cause of Downside's failure.

At the time that Angus McPhee made his dramatic appearance, things had reached such a stage that they could not be much worse. Either the Club had to be disbanded, or there would have to be a drastic improvement. After holding out for three months, the last of a long, but not illustrious, line of trainers, had turned in his toes, packed his spare shirt, and vanished into space, thankful to leave the town with his life. Circumstances, in which he profanely included Mr. Horace Ovens, had been too much for him.

Which brings us at last to Mr. Ovens.

Mr. Horace Ovens had the largest waistband, the emptiest mind, and the foulest tongue in modern professional football. Only a perverse fate had stopped him from being born a German, and rising to sergeant-major rank in the pre-war Prussian Guards. He was not so much a man as a warning.

His official position was Secretary-Manager. He had come to the Club the last year Downside were in the First Division. It was significant and characteristic of the man that the Club dropped to the Second Division the following season – and stayed on in the darkness. It would probably have dropped into the Third Division, but for the fact that was no Third Division, then.

Mr. Ovens would, no doubt, have called himself a disciplinarian had he known the meaning of the word, whereas he was nothing but a bully. No self-respecting player could allow himself to be spoken to as Ovens invariably wanted to speak to him. The result was that no sooner did Downside a promising player, than they lost him. He applied at once to be placed on the open-to-transfer list. If this request were refused he played so badly that he had to be dispensed with. Newcastle United, Tottenham Hotspur, Middlesbrough, Liverpool – to name a few leading clubs – secured such players, and generally made "stars" out of them. Others who remained cursed their fate, so ably did Mr. Horace Ovens fulfil his duties.

It was never properly understood why the directors tolerated Ovens. Some said that the Rangers, the successful rival team of the town, subscribed to the Downside funds on the understanding that Ovens was not dismissed. This was the jocular cynical view.

Ovens was a man with the ability of impressing others with his own importance. The directors had allowed him to dominate them all completely. Even the chairman, Benjamin Fortey, was notoriously afraid of him. Add to this the fact that Ovens had some money invested in the Club, more than the directors could afford to pay out, and that he worked for a salary which no self-respecting football team manager would have accepted, and his continued residence at Downside is explained.

Horace Ovens was a widower. He had a waspish daughter, the unlovely Una, who had married a printer on the staff of the local evening paper, *The Downside Echo*, and Jim Panes had the mortification of providing board and lodging for the most unpopular man in the town.

On the night of the coming of McPhee as Panes sat at supper, the heavy step of his father-in-law was heard in the narrow hall. Later his father-in-law and "paying-guest" as his daughter always expressed it, entered the room. He was a man with a broad expanse of clean-shaven face, the lips of which were contorted into a perpetual smirk.

No one had ever seen him without that smirk, which was as false as a painted hussy's smile. He smirked at all hours of the day – smirked when he shaved, when he ate, drank; smirked more than ever when he cursed an unfortunate player or the groundsman. He was smirking now as he entered, although he had just returned from a fruitless journey to sign on an outside right.

Next to the smirk, the most noticeable features about the Downside manager were a bulging body, a blatant almost-gold watch-chain, the too many rings (one on each *middle* finger) and the unpleasant voice.

'Well, Jim, my boy, what's doing? 'he demanded, flinging his hat and overcoat on the sofa, and seating himself at the table.

Panes winced. He was a weak character, willing at all times to sacrifice himself for peace.

'The Club's got a new trainer,' he replied with his mouth full. 'I heard the yarn in the office this afternoon. The fellow's mad, I think. Says he is going to teach Downside to play football scientifically.'

Horace Ovens gazed at his son-in-law, the smirk almost disappearing in his amazement. 'Going to teach 'em to play football scientifically is he!' he repeated, and smirked – most dreadfully. 'I wonder what he's goin' to teach me, and what I'm goin' to teach *him*, blast him! Why the hell can't you pass the pickles, Jim?' he demanded a moment later.

CHAPTER III

MCPHEE GETS BUSY

On the morning following his official appointment – Wednesday – the new trainer of the Downside Club rose early, had a cold bath, went through his customary dumb-bell exercises, and did some earnest and consistent thinking. All these things were characteristic of the man.

In spite of his odd appearance and his quaint mannerisms, Angus McPhee was far from being a fool. Psychologists might have said that he was a little mad, but most men with missions have been a little mad. McPhee had played football as a boy, but on reaching the age of seventeen, he had, after the fashion of so many of his race, become so absorbed in work that he had had no time to spare on anything but business. At an early age he had been apprenticed to the grocery trade in a shop on the outskirts of Glasgow. A tyrannous employer had sweated the life out of him (McPhee had lived on the premises), and when the assistant became, in the course of time, manager of the business, McPhee had grown so accustomed to working the clock round that he knew no other life than that of abject slavery and incessant drudgery.

War, acted as an earthquake to him; it changed a pallid cheesemonger into a MAN! On the night of August 4th, 1914, McPhee had heard the pipers playing their soul-stirring music in a Glasgow street – and the next morning found the grocery manager missing: Angus McPhee had discarded the bacon-knife for the bayonet, having enlisted 3 a.m. in the morning in the 5th Scottish Unbendables.

The successive hells through which he passed held no terrors for the former grocery slave. In the past, life had possessed no meaning for Angus McPhee; now the fierce tang of his new existence contained endless joys. He became first the butt and then the pride of his sergeant-major; he learned everything quickly because he wanted to get all he could out of this strange throbbing life into which he had been pitchforked.

Angus McPhee made a queer recruit – but a magnificent soldier. He looked the most miserable man in the British Army, but in reality he was the happiest.

After the grocer's shop war was a beautiful, if terrible, thing. He flung himself into everything with a splendid abandon; finding his once-miserable body respond to the hard training, he gloried in keeping himself in the pink of condition. He became as hard and wiry as a mountain goat.

In between the fighting there was football. Only a man who had lived the existence of McPhee – starved of everything which gladdens the pageant of life – could have taken up the game with the boyish, almost childish, enthusiasm that he showed. Twenty long years seemed to fall off his shoulders: he was a ragged-trousered youngster again, kicking a tin about the waste ground at the back of his poor home.

A bullet through the left knee stopped him from playing football himself, but even this reverse did not daunt him. He promptly flung all his passion for the game into "management." Seeing the type he was, his officers handed over the sole direction of the regimental team to Sergeant Angus McPhee.

"Mad McPhee," as they affectionately called him, moulded the players to his will. He was their father, mother and family doctor. He had evolved his own views about the game, and these he imparted to his charges. The result was that the 5th Scottish Unbendables went through the rest of the Brigade football teams like a scythe through corn and in the end were acclaimed the finest regimental team throughout the B.E.F!

By this time, the game had become a religion with this wonder-trainer, who was accounted too good to be really true. His fame spread through the armed camps of France like a flaming legend. In the 5th Scottish Unbendables, if there were a difficult of work to be done, the sovereign remedy as to hand it over to McPhee. So much fame had the man achieved.

Because he loved the life, McPhee stayed on in the Service for as long as he could. Letters which were sent him by the proprietor of the grocery store in the suburb of Glasgow, recalling him to his now hated task, were torn up – after he had replied tersely to the effect that he had no intention of taking up the bacon knife again.

When McPhee was at length demobilised, he was a sad being. Long before this his beloved football team had vanished – scattered apparently to the four ends of the earth.

Once more his life seemed empty. There was only his vastly improved health and a tremendously different outlook to remind him of those hard yet happy years of the War.

He became sadder still when he found that there was no place for him in the world to which he had come back. It was impossible for him to contemplate returning to the only job he knew – managing a grocer's shop.

It was not until he had touched the rock-bottom of Despair that the one genuine inspiration of his life came to him. Professional football enthusiasm was at full flood; much of the play was deplorable – why couldn't he do in civil life what he had done in the Army?

It seemed simple enough at first, especially in view of his certificates showing that he had practical experience of massage and the human anatomy. Then there was his Army record behind him; but he had a sad disillusionment when he came to put the idea to a practical test.

He had never mastered the art of dressing himself without accentuating his gaunt characteristics. His amazing hats and black woollen gloves (relics of his stern Scottish upbringing) caused ribaldry rather than confidence. The queer way he had of stating his views, much after the fashion of a revivalist expounding a new, and yet old, religious creed, completed the impression that the War somehow had turned his head. Disappointment followed disappointment. Most of the big clubs were already fixed up with chief and assistant trainers, and the fact he had had no actual experience with a professional team was a fatal handicap.

"Army football!" the average manager would scoff. "Why, that's kick-tin! No, sorry – but we might be able to offer you something as a groundsman, perhaps…"

Possessed by the restless ambition to show a football team how to play better than any other team was playing at the sent time, McPhee would not compromise. He would not level his standard, or sacrifice his ideal. If he could not be a properly-appointed and recognised trainer he would pass on. He passed on – until he came to rest at Downside. By this time he had spent practically all his savings (including his gratuity) and had travelled many hundreds of miles. In places where they talked football he was already known as "the sawny Scotsman." Perhaps it was a hasty verdict.

After breakfasting at the small temperance hotel in which he had temporarily pitched his tent, McPhee walked to the ground which was to be at once his workshop and his factory for the next month at least. He had no need to ask his way, for he had been in the town since the previous Saturday when Downside, after an atrocious and humiliating exhibition of football, had lost 3-0 to Hilltown Athletic.

He had been told by the chairman of the Club that the players were supposed to report for training at ten o'clock in the morning, but he was on the ground by twenty minutes past nine. He wished to make himself familiar with his surroundings before commencing operations.

An uncouth individual, standing at the large red-painted gate that opened on to an asphalt track, stared at him as he approached, and barred the way.

'No admittance 'ere!' he announced brusquely. 'This is the Downside football ground, and it's private!'

'Is that a fact?' said McPhee: 'Well, I'm no exactly a stranger: I'm the new trainer.'

The loutish groundsman opened his mouth wide, surveyed the speaker from head to foot, and then guffawed.

'Sure you ain't a barber's pole?' he inquired and perhaps would have added more, when suddenly a long lean arm shot out, and the hand at the end of it caught groundsman by one shoulder and swirled him round as though he had been on a wire.

'I dinna want any mair o' that frae ye,' cut in a voice that had the hiss of steel and the whip of whalebone in it, 'havena' I telt ye I'm the new trainer?'

The facetious groundsman had been in a labour battalion in the years that were past, and he recognised the tone as that of a competent and self-reliant N.C.O. There could no fooling this fellow, he decided, although he looked like nothing on earth.

'You'll want the dressin-rooms, I -suppose,' he said. 'Round to the right, beneath the grand-stand. Door's marked Players Only!' he vouchsafed, and McPhee released his hold.

'Ye'll ken me anither time,' he said pleasantly, and he went his way, the grounds-man staring after him as though he were a vision.

There was no difficulty about getting into the dressing-rooms, for he had been given a key. The equipment was good, but sadly neglected; the baths were grimy, and the floor of the rooms littered with refuse.

It went straight to the new trainer's heart to see this neglect in a place which should have been as spotless as a hotel bathroom, and he found himself a job at once. Turning on the water in the big plunge bath, he commenced to scrub the sides and bottom.

Then, leaving the water running, he went for assistance. Outside in the corridor he almost cannoned into the groundsman.

'Whose job is it to keep the floor clean?' he demanded. 'If its yours ye'd better get stairted to it.'

The groundsman had help. With his coat off, and his shirt-sleeves rolled up, McPhee did most of the work himself, but he saw to it that the other did not idle.

They had just completed the task when a number of men strolled languidly into the nearest room.

'Guid mornin', lads,' said McPhee, handing over his broom to the groundsman, who took it with a scowl.

'Who d'you think you are?' grunted the first of the Downside players.

'The new trainer,' came the unruffled response; 'I'll be wi' ye in a minute!'

The man who had asked the question emitted a long shrill whistle, eloquent of many qualities, including delighted wonder, and the determination to make the most of this good thing which had come his way. As a prospective taskmaster, this extreme lengthy, sandy-topped, sad-visaged individual promised to be a sheer joy.

McPhee paid no attention, either to the whistle or to the expectant grins which greeted it. He did not expect this job of his to be easy; much of the zest would have already gone from it if that had proved to be the case. That he would receive jeers, sniggers and other marks of contumely from the players who were in his charge for at least a month was to be expected; indeed, it was inevitable. It was his fate to be laughed at on a first meeting.

That was all part of the job, however; he didn't mind, he had grown accustomed to it. Professional footballers were like grown-up boys in many ways; he would manage them in time.

At that moment someone whom the new trainer had not included in his calculations stood in the doorway, shutting out the sunlight.

He wore a profusion of jewellery, too much stomach, and too much smirk. It was Mr. Horace Ovens come to perform his well-known act of "wind-up." The new trainer was his objective.

He waddled forward, his narrow eyes mere slits. At his feet yapped a couple of self-important toy-dogs.

'Why aren't you changed?' he demanded, glaring round at the Downside players, who had risen from the lockers on which they had been lazily lounging.

It was at this moment that Angus McPhee moved forward. A couple of his long strides brought him to the side of the orbicular Ovens.

'The men have juist come. It's only five minutes past ten. They'll be oot in the field shortly,' he said.

The globular manager glowered up at the speaker. 'Who the flaming 'ell are you?' he erupted. It was his obvious intention to intimidate and humiliate the man before the players over whom he had control.

'My name is McPhee – Angus McPhee,' replied the other quietly. 'I'm the new trainer of the Club – and one o' my rules is that I'll have no swearin' in the dressin'-room.'

There was dead silence for a few seconds. The Downside players were staring at one another, scarcely daring to trust their ears, while

Ovens gasped in his endeavour to recover his poise. It was the calm before the storm; an explosion was imminent and inevitable.

When it came, it was terrific. Ovens, master of devastating invective, surpassed himself, introducing several new and completely novel oaths. Even the oldest Downside player in the room had never heard anything like it. This was Ovens' dreadful best, and it was all directed at McPhee.

The eyes of the room were upon the latter. He smiled through the storm — smiled in a way that would have conveyed volumes to any of his old comrades in the 6th Scottish Unbendables.

When Ovens had finally slackened through sheer want of breath, McPhee made a significant reply.

'Ye don't seem to believe me; but I've already telt ye I'm the new trainer of the Club… Ach, mon, I should have warned ye to be careful…'

There was a mighty splash, and then a series of sounds that an expiring whale might have made. After that, an explosion of laughter from the watching Downside players.

How it had happened no one could say, but there was Horace Ovens, the man they all hated, plopping about full-stretch in the great plunge-bath. Completely clothed, as he was, even to his bowler-hat, he presented a picture which was both memorable and lasting.

'Ye'll droon yoursel', mon, if ye're not careful,' said McPhee, whose face had never lost its habitual gravity.

Stooping, he clutched the whale-like form of Ovens, picking him easily and cleanly out of the water.

'Ye've juist about spoilt the water,' he added, looking critically at the contents of the bath. 'But you'll want your hat.' Retrieving the manager's ruined bowler, he rammed it, dripping wet as it was, down upon Ovens' bullet head. It was the finishing touch.

'You pushed me in — you pushed me in!' screamed the soaking manager.'

Pushed ye in!' repeated McPhee incredulously. 'Me push ye in! What are ye talkin' aboot, mon? Pushed ye in! As though I should do such a thing to the manager of the Club. I thought ye were going to fall, and I tried to catch hold of ye — but you were in the bath before I could grab ye. It was a bad business — but an accident for a' that.'

Horace Ovens' rage choked him. He was unable to make any reply.'

'If ye'll take off your wet claothes, I'll gi'e ye a rub doon,' continued McPhee, self-possessed and unruffled. 'Now, lads,' turning to the mesmerised Downside players, 'we'll have a wee bit o' talk together, you and I. It's juist as well that we should thoroughly onderstand each other before we stairt.'

CHAPTER IV

SHOWING THEM HOW

'Sit doon,' said McPhee. 'Lads,' he resumed: 'it's necessary that we should be friends; that's why I said juist now that we must thoroughly onderstand each ither. We ha'e a stiff job in front of us, and the only way to do it is by pullin' all togither. It's team-work that counts.

'I'm goin' to talk straight to ye, lads, this mornin'. That's the only way we can get to know each ither – by talkin' straight. I saw ye play last Saturday, and ye're about the worst team I've iver seen. Now don't look fierce, for it's juist the plain truth that I'm tellin' ye.'

'Well? 'said a voice, challengingly.

'By admittin' it, ye show ye've got some sense, onyway. Now, I take it ye don't want to remain the worst team? No weel that's perfectly natural. Within a month, if ye work hard and do what I want ye to do, ye'll no' be the worst team in country. I've no had charge of a professional team before, but I've got my own ideas about football – peculiar some of them may be –'

'Are you the McPhee who trained the 5th Scottish Unbendables in France?' asked a voice.

'Aye, I'm the same mon.'

'H'm!' The player lapsed into silence again without further questions or comment.

'It's a deep hole that we're in – you, because you're worst team in the country, and me because I ha'e to train ye. But if we pull together we shall get oot of it; remember that… Now, if yell get changed, lads, we can feenish our talk later on.'

'He's barmy!' whispered Jimmy Nixon convincingly.

'That's what they said in the Unbendables,' replied Tommy Trott, who had asked McPhee the question. He did not complete the sentence, but chuckled exasperatingly.

The Downside players changed silently into their training garb. They were badly shaken.

'Get your boots on, lads,' said McPhee. 'Ball practice to-day. Ye canna' hope to play football until ye lairn to trap the ball – nobody can. Ball practice – makin' the ball do what you want it to do – is the essence of football.'

Through sheer force of habit, and not because he felt any special resentment against the man who had given the order, Sam Simister, the registered buffoon of the team, leaned forward.

'I'll bet *you're* some conjurer, old college chum' he grinned.

'Weel,' replied McPhee judicially, as he commenced to undress; 'I've a wee limp in the left leg; but ask no mon to do what I canna' do mysel'.'

He picked up the ball as he spoke, and performed the trick which he had shown the night before to the astounded directors of the Club.

'The essence of football is ball control,' he reiterated, as he flung the football aside and went on with his own changing. The words were to become the slogan of the Downside Football Club.

The eyes of the players opened wider than ever. McPhee dressed in street clothes was an oddity; McPhee in football attire was a sight for gods and sporting cartoonists. Tom Webster would have danced round him in an ecstasy of delight. Never had an English professional football dressing-room contained such a spectacle. His legs were like elongated exclamation marks.

He noticed the smiles, and his eyes twinkled. There something appealing about the man, ridiculous as he looked. The players had already had some experience of the manner in which he met a crisis, and handled a situation.

'Ye'll be thinkin' what a sicht I am?' McPhee commented, and the sadness which was seemingly part of his nature enveloped him. In that moment, Angus McPhee had the lock of a lonesome man.

'But we're wastin' time!' he cried, suddenly.

He picked up several practice balls that were lying about and led the way out of the dressing-room.

Out on the playing pitch, the Downside players received even further surprises. They had thought the new trainer was boasting when he had said he knew what to do with a football. But he did! He proved he could trap a ball with the deftness of a Robert Kelly[1], and shoot with an accuracy and power that was literally flabbergasting. Although he was lame, he could get a ball under instant control and shoot without hesitation with his one sound leg.

---

[1] Robert Kelly was former miner turned footballer who played for Burnley around the time of the First World War. He helped them to win the First Division in 1920-21 and scored 88 goals in 277 games for the club, In 1925 he transferred to Sunderland for a record fee of £6,550. He was capped for England 14 times scoring 7 goals.

Here was a practical man, and the Downside players were forced to recognise him as such. They forgot the eccentric appearance of this new trainer, who had apparently sprung up out of the ground, in the fascination of watching him do the things they were paid to do, but did not do.

'Now watch, boys,' said McPhee.

He was perfectly happy and completely absorbed. On the other side of the railings which surrounded the playing pitch were a number of idlers, who had been drawn inside by the irresistible appeal which a football bouncing upon turf exerts. They were gibing at the new trainer's spare and attenuated form, but McPhee was indifferent to everything but the job he had on hand. He revelled in it, putting into it the enthusiasm of youth, and the iron determination of his own grim character.

He placed the ball twenty yards from the goal-line, and prepared to kick.

'I'll ha'e ye to know that I shall aim juist inside the left post,' he said, as though giving a lecture. 'You, lad,' addressing the goalkeeper, 'are welcome to that wee bit o' information. Now – see!'

He hobbled awkwardly forward. His boot met the ball in a dull thud. Although it had been stationary, the ball tumbled forward with the velocity of a bullet. There was something more than velocity; there was uncanny accuracy. It sped as straight as an arrow's flight to that part of the goal at which McPhee had said he would direct it.

The regular Downside first team custodian had sprung to the left, but the force of the shot beat him, and the ball shook the back of the net.

'Ye canna' expect to do onything in football unless ye take pains,' said McPhee, turning round. 'Practice makes pairfect, they say, and that's aboot the truest thing they ever did say. What ye have to get oot of your heads is that the popular kind of trainin' is all right instead of all wrong. Any fule can run fast – but it takes more than speed to make a football player. So long as I am the trainer of this Club, ye'll ha'e to play football, not win sprints.

'We shall try stunts – I'm a good moon at stunts – that'll put some bonus money in your pooches about Christmas-time. But we'll ha'e to work together: we've got to have confidence in each ither. And now let's get to work.'

The Downside players were thinking hard as they returned to their dressing-room two hours later. They were annoyed with themselves. They wanted to dislike this fellow who acknowledged he was a human freak, but they found it impossible. By all the rules and regulations they should have already commenced to make the life of the new trainer a "merry hell"; yet no one seemed to know exactly how to start. What was more, every man deep down in his heart, would have felt ashamed if any of the others *had* started. The fellow might be a freak — but he was certainly a man.

At that moment the same thought seemed to strike several of the returning players, who began to laugh.

'What's the joke aboot, lads?' McPhee seemed to know, however, that the laugh was not against himself.

It was Tommy Trott, the inside-right, who replied.

'I can't help thinking of Ovens!' he cried. 'You know, I suppose,' he added, turning to McPhee, 'that Ovens is the biggest swine in football. Hanging is too good for him!'

'Do ye ken that partial droonin' will do the trick?' replied the trainer with a flitting smile. 'I can see mysel' what sort o' mon yon is. But I'm no such a fule to run out against the mon in authority over me.'

The players reflected on this.

'He'll make the town too hot to hold you after what happened this morning.' Said one.

'No mon can read the future, lad; an' in ony case, I'll no' permit sweerin' in the dressin'-room.'

Having said so much, the new trainer of Downside retired into silence.

CHAPTER V

THE MATTER OF A MASCOT

It was Joe Tranter, the outside-right of the team, who started the subject, half-an-hour later.

'What this Club wants,' he said decisively, 'is a mascot! We haven't had a bit of luck since the taxi ran over our black kitten. You've got no objection to a mascot, I suppose?' the winger continued, looking fixedly at McPhee.

The latter studied his man. Tranter was a shock-headed, swarthy-complexioned, sullen-browed youth, who looked as though he were engaged in a conspiracy against the whole world. McPhee had met the type in the Army – brooding, superstitious, inclined to be resentful of all authority, or criticism – a difficult fellow to handle.

'Yes! let's get a mascot for Saturday!' chimed in a supporting voice. 'It's a fact,' corroborated this speaker, 'that we haven't had a bit of luck since the black kitten we found in the dressing-room one morning and adopted was run over by a taxi just outside the entrance. It was one of those damnation dogs of Ovens' that made her run away and get killed!' The player snarled in his bitterness.

'Good morning all!' said a cheery voice at the door. McPhee turned instantly in that direction, but the greetings of the players were given without turning their backs.

'Mornin', "Happy"!'

'What, you up already, you fat, lazy devil?' 'Come along in, can't you?' 'Well, how's the best football writer in Downside this morning?'

These and half a dozen other welcomes were flung at the newcomer. Whoever this man might be, McPhee knew that he was "a member of the same lodge" as the Downside players.

He looked at the man with added interest. He saw a round, happy-looking face, carelessly shaven and topped by a pair of eyeglasses which were so insecurely fixed to the wearer's nose that they looked like falling off at any moment; a stoutish frame clad in a seedy, threadbare overcoat beneath which showed much-worn, baggy trousers and regrettable boots. A rusty-looking bowler hat and a cherry-wood walking stick, crooked over the left arm, completed the picture. As McPhee looked across at him, the eyes behind the precarious eyeglasses twinkled, flashing a friendly greeting at him.

'Morning,' the stranger said again, this time addressing himself directly to McPhee.

The trainer smiled back.

'Come along in,' he said warmly, repeating the words of Tommy Trott.

The latter rose to the occasion. ' "Happy", ' he said, catching hold of the stranger's arm, and guiding him over to McPhee, 'this is our new trainer, McPhee – and this,' pushing an elbow affectionately into the chest of his convoy, 'is Mr. Howard – "Happy" Howard, as everyone calls him in this town. A real good sort; all the boys like him – even if he is a terrible football writer! '

'Very pleased to meet you, Mr. McPhee,' said the journalist, his eyes twinkling more than ever. 'I'm on the *Downside Evening Echo*, and but for being out of town yesterday I should have interviewed you, and given you a welcome to Downside.'

'I'm verra pleased to meet you!' replied McPhee, giving the extended hand a hearty grip. He liked this reporter on sight: the man looked a sportsman.

'I saw Mr. Ovens just now; he seemed put out about something,' remarked Happy, smiling broadly.

The Downside players wriggled in their seats like a flock of mischievous schoolboys. They laughed and looked towards McPhee.

But the latter disappointed them. 'Mr. Howard,' he said solemnly, 'I feel that I can trust ye. That is why I am going to tell ye aboot what happened to Mr. Ovens this mornin'. The facts are not for publication, ye onderstand?

'I understand, Mr. McPhee,' replied the reporter, although he wondered why the more serious the new trainer became, the more the Downside players grinned.

'Ye'll onderstand, Mr. Howard,' the trainer continued, when he had come to the end of the narrative, 'that I'm tellin' ye this because I want ye to get the real facts at first-hand, and no imaginary facts at second-hand.'

'Quite; and I thank you for giving me that confidence. Now, is there any way in which I can be of service to you in return?'

The trainer smiled.

'These lads,' indicating the Downside players, 'thought the Club ought to have a wee mascot. Now I'll ask ye – would that gi'e ye sornethin' to write aboot in your newspaper?'

'It certainly would, and,' with a smile which was perfectly guileless, 'there is no doubt this team wants *something!* It hasn't been all bad play, however, that has landed the Club at the bottom of the Second Division.'

'That's what I say, "Happy",' cried Joe Tranter, springing from his seat, and taking the centre of the stage. 'Last night it came to me all of a sudden!' he cried, waving his hands, 'we've been playing under a spell – somebody's "wished" something on us! If we had a mascot, we should begin to win matches. What about it?' He flung the challenge to the trainer.

McPhee had, in the ordinary way, little sympathy with "supersteetious haverings." His experience had been that only hard work – and plenty of it – wrought miracles, or anything approaching miracles. He was a Scot, and he faced facts in the dour Caledonian manner.

But all the same he knew that he would lose nothing, and perhaps might gain a great deal, by falling in with Tranter's suggestion.

'Richt! If ye'll make up your minds, lads, ye shall ha'e a mascot. Will ye leave it to me to get ye one.'

His words were greeted with enthusiasm.

'We'll leave it to you – only get a good 'un!' cried one.

McPhee's grim features twisted themselves into a smile.

'We'll ha'e to buy the mascot between us, lads,' he said. 'I'm Scotch; but it's in a good cause!' He put a ten shilling note into the bowler which "Happy" Howard held out.

It was a good example. The players had been paid the day before, and they still had some money left. Silver literally rained into the hat.

'Four pounds eighteen and sixpence,' announced the reporter, after he had poured it out and counted the pile of silver. 'There goes the socks I ought to have bought,' he said, adding half-a-crown out of his pocket to the rest. 'And now what?'

'I'm juist gain' to gi'e the lads a receipt for their money,' said McPhee.

'That's all right!' called out the club inside-right: 'You aren't going to run away, are you?'

'Not for a month,' was the reply.

'I'll be lookin' to ye to help me over this, Mr. Howard.'

The morning practice was over; the dressing-room had been tidied; the players were gone; and McPhee and his new acquaintance, *The Echo* sporting reporter, were walking towards the entrance gates of the ground.

'You can depend on me, Mr. McPhee,' replied the reporter. 'I want you to know at the start that I'm out to help you all I can.'

By this time the pair were walking past the office of the Club, which was situated by the entrance gates. Through one of the windows they saw the manager glaring at them balefully.

'Its not for me to poke my nose into things which aren't my concern, Mr. McPhee, but I know from experience that that man is not too pleasant a character,' remarked the reporter; 'you'll take that the right way, I hope?'

'Ye'll ken I know that already, Mr. Howard; but I thank ye all the same for the warnin'. It shows ye're goin' to be a friend to me. I'm thinkin' that I'll be mighty short of friends soon; not that I've ever had many friends.' And again that wistful look of a lonesome man passed over his face.

'You left them all in France, perhaps,' continued the reporter, putting a hand on the other's arm; 'a cousin of mine – a dear kid; he's buried in the Flanders mud, God rest him! – was in your battalion of the 5th Scottish Unbendables in France, and he wrote home and told me all about you. He described you so minutely that I knew you must be the same man directly I saw you this morning. You were everything that was wonderful to that kid – you saved him body and soul once... if you want my friendship, such as it is, you can have it – or anything else!'

'Your friendship will be enough, I'm thinkin' – and there's nae doubt but what I shall value it,' said McPhee quietly, and, for the second time that morning, he shook the hand which was outstretched to him.

'But aboot the mascot; I ha'e a fancy for something oreeginal: an animal, if possible. Now, where can I buy an animal that is oreeginal?'

'Here, jump on this car; we'll go to Trimble's,' said the reporter. Ten minutes later McPhee found himself entering an evil-smelling shop over which in dingy lettering was the announcement that Joshua Trimble was a naturalist and bird fancier.

Mr. Joshua Trimble was a lean, lantern-jawed old gentleman in a skull-cap, carpet slippers, a cockney accent, and an unmistakable aroma.

He looked at the deputation from the Downside Football Club and rubbed his thin hands.

'A mascot?' he repeated; 'why, cert'nly I can sell you a mascot. Anyfink from a flea to an elerphant In course the larst would come pretty dear,' he added. . . 'What's your fancy?'

"Happy" Howard beamed in characteristic fashion.

'What's the present fashion?' he inquired. 'A fellow might as well be dead as be out of the fashion.'

'The present fashion in mascots,' replied Mr. Trimble oracularly, 'is goats. Goats, in fact, are *the* thing at the present toime. If yer takes my advice you'll 'ave a goat.'

'A goat!' repeated McPhee. 'We'll see him.'

The goat who was fated to play such an important part in the future destinies of the Downside players proved to be a sagacious-looking animal bearing such a remarkable resemblance to some of the old Biblical Kings that Howard at once said his only possible name could be "Neb" – short for Nebuchadnezzar.

'Yes, gen'l'men, there's your mascot.' Mr. Trimble rambled on. 'All the best people are having goats just now. This week I've sent off three – two to crack regiments, and one to a battleship.'

McPhee took a long, comprehensive look at the goat. He did not disclose what passed through his mind, but brought the business to a close by inquiring, 'Hoo much?'

Five minutes later, Mr. Trimble had acquired the dressing- room collection and McPhee found himself tethered to a goat with a speculative eye and a workmanlike pair of horns.

So the deed was done. Neb changed owners, and entered upon his duties as mascot straightaway.

Out into the crowded Market Street the strange couple marched, the new mascot of the Downside Football Club attracting all the attention he deserved. Business, as represented by those Hercules of activity, the errand-boys of the town, was soon at a standstill. It was only when Nebuchadnezzar bared his teeth in a particularly ghastly grin that the police were able to move the crowd on.

'I must get back and write this!' said Howard, tensely, 'the story may make the town laugh – but it will add five thousand to the "gate" on Saturday!' To himself, he added, 'I wonder what Nancy will say about McPhee?'

He hurried away, chuckling.

CHAPTER VI

NEB'S FOUL

"Happy" Howard, football writer and good fellow, may not have known much about the "nice conduct of a clouded cane," or the latest method of pressing trousers, but give him a pencil, place some paper before him, and he was working at his trade. That night when Downside sat down to its tea, it had something piquant to digest with the kippers –

NEW TRAINER'S FIRST ACT.
BUYS MASCOT FOR DOWNSIDE FOOTBALL CLUB.
YOU CAN'T GET
ANGUS McPHEE'S GOAT!

That evening Downside allowed its kippers to grow cold while it read on –

> "Of late Downside Football Club has had bad luck; in fact, ever since the present season started. But, if the Fates are kind, all this is going to be altered; not only have the Club a new trainer – a man who has already shown that he is a master of an extremely difficult job – *but the team has acquired a mascot!*
>
> "On behalf of the Downside players, Mr. Angus McPhee, the new trainer for the Downside Club, purchased this afternoon from Mr. Trimble, the well-known local animal dealer, a "guaranteed lucky" goat. According to Mr. Trimble, goats lead the present-day fashion in mascots, and are, moreover, notoriously lucky. May it prove so!
>
> "We understand that the most exhaustive preparations are being made to give the luck of Nebuchadnezzar – for so the new mascot of the Downside has been named – a fair run for its money. Neb is to be given a coat of Club colours – *viz.* red and white – which he will wear at the home match with Bankpark Albion on Saturday,

and all those things which are fit and proper for a goat to have shall be his. All he has to do in return is to prove his real worth as a mascot."

Downside laughed – as who would not laugh at the idea of a football club depending on a mascot when its own play was so bad that it couldn't seem to help itself? It laughed again – more cheerfully, humanly, and agreeably this time – when it conjured up the picture of a full-sized goat in a uniform of red and white flannel. It decided to turn up and see the vision. Which was what was desired. The Downside Football Club was in a position of wanting a crowd by any means which might be employed. Harassed by debt, the directors would have welcomed a "gate" of twenty thousand with mingled astonishment and gratified blasphemy.

Ten thousand of that crowd were to be seen in the flesh on the following Saturday. The majority had come to see what they called "The Circus," and not the football; but the main point is that they paid over their shillings and half-crowns. It was confidently expected that Bankpark Albion would smother Downside to the extent of at least three clear goals – but there was the goat to be seen.

It took some time to prepare Neb for the historic occasion. Joe Tranter, with the aid of the rest of the team, strove manfully to garb Neb in his mascot's uniform. It was a long job, and in the process the right-winger was badly winded.

It had been decided that the captain of the Downside team should lead the goat out ceremoniously when the team took the field, and then hand it over to McPhee, who, sitting on the trainer's bench just inside the railings, would look after Neb throughout the game. Practically everyone on the ground would be able to see that the goat was really a mascot and not a mere newspaper yarn.

The yell that went up from that crowd of ten thousand onlookers when they caught the first glimpse of Neb, wrapped up in his flannel jacket, made the ramshackle smaller grandstand rock on its foundations. It was a memorable moment for the Club, its supporters and for Neb. Nothing in Neb's sweet young life had ever stirred him as this did. As though sensing the mood of the company, he commenced capering to the extravagant delight of the crowd. The only expression Joe Tranter, in whose head had been this notion of mascotry, could give of his joy was to snatch the leather leash and join Neb in a wonderful *pas de deux*. But for the appearance of the referee, this would undoubtedly have been encored.

Breathlessly the crowd watched the two captains tossing. Would the Downside mascot thus early give a demonstration of his powers? A terrific roar greeted the fact that the home skipper had guessed rightly the call of the coin.

Up in the directors' box, Horace Ovens watched the proceedings with a bilious eye. He had said nothing about Neb, and had taken the precaution of keeping out of range of his horned rushes. He had received one shock to his nervous system, and he wanted time to recover. In the meantime – so he told himself – "he was giving the fool the rope to 'ang 'imself with." But he promised himself that his satisfaction should not suffer through the self-imposed waiting.

In the meantime, the game had started with the Downside players frolicking like young colts. The example set by Neb was contagious; they went about their business with so much light-hearted abandon that the crowd scarcely recognised them. Listlessness had given way to energy, indifference to zest. Within the first five minutes they almost scored!

The wheezes of Mr. Samuel Spurgeon, the heaviest football official in England, told of the excitement which was ranging in the directors' box. For the first time that season, Downside looked like qualifying for a bonus. On the right wing Tranter was playing like a man who had caught fire – running like the wind, and sending red-hot shots in from almost any angle. That these failed to score was due to marvellous work by the Albion's goalkeeper. Once Tranter followed up a shot with such rapidity that he nearly bundled both man and ball over the line. Instantly his hands sprang into the air in passionate appeal.

The referee shook his head, and waved Tranter away – both signs of negation – and although the crowd, with characteristic frankness, told him that they had seen better things come out of cheese, he still refused to allow the goal. Walking back to the touch-line with arms folded moodily, a veritable footballing Hamlet, Tranter brooded darkly.

The crowd soon simmered down. For one thing, the refusal of the referee to allow that debatable goal had taken the edge off the home team's impetuosity; while, for another, the danger which had been so narrowly averted had roused their opponents to a sense of their responsibilities. Bankpark Albion were standing third in the League table, and were hopeful of climbing yet higher. From the next goal-kick they attacked like swarming bees.

Football, like life, goes by extremes. For the first ten minutes of the game Downside over-ran their opponents; now their opponents were over-running them. For five minutes the raiders were arrested, and then –

It happened in this fashion: the centre-half rushed in to tackle, got the ball from the Downside centre-forward, and banged it out to the left. Taking it in his stride, the winger tricked the half, and full-back, and cut in. Gerrish, the Downside left back, rushed across in a desperate effort to save the situation; but before he could tackle the winger, the latter had swung the ball across the goal-mouth to the Albion centre-forward.

It seemed that nothing could prevent a goal. Quinn, the Albion centre-forward, had the reputation of being the deadliest shot in the Second Division. It was impossible that he would miss a gift like that. The crowd hung mesmerised over the railings. They saw Quinn nudge the ball on a bit before letting fly; they saw him prepare to shoot, and then–

From the direction of the grand-stand had started a gale of laughter. It spread all over the ground. Men shouted. Women shrilled.

Those who had turned away, feeling certain (and sick, in consequence) that Quinn would score, looked again – and then they, too, joined in the chorus.

Just as Quinn was about to shoot – just at the moment that his dreaded right foot was seen to leave the ground – he was charged from behind by Neb, the new Downside mascot!

Tearing across the field he had come, the highest-minded he-goat in captivity, doing a job of work to earn his keep! He charged Quinn amidships – and the ball went soaring over the bar, miles too high!

Quinn went face first into the mud.

'Penalty!' he screamed, and the crowd became helpless. Even the Albion players joined in: the thought of a penalty against a goat was irresistibly funny.

'Where *is* he?' demanded Quinn, clambering to his feet and spitting the mud from his mouth.

'There he is!'

The openly, flagrantly jubilant Joe Tranter pointed to Neb, who seemed bent upon performing other startling acts of mascotry.

'It's our mascot!' Tranter explained.

By the time the Albion centre-forward had digested this amazing item of news, the referee had recovered and pointed for a goal-kick.

Hopping mad, Quinn turned and tried a headlong kick at the Downside mascot; but the turf was treacherous, and the centre's boot never reached its objective. Thus for the second time within a short space, Quinn bit the mud – quite a lot of mud.

'Easy there 'breathed the Downside outside-right in the prostrate one's ear; 'Old Neb's sacred – he's eleven hundred and forty-nine years old, and he ain't to be touched!'

In the meanwhile the Downside penalty area was like a revivalist meeting. All the Bankpark players were appealing to the referee to see the light – in other words, to give the penalty kick to which they maintained they were entitled.

But the referee continued to point for a goal-kick. He was firm, although he trembled. In his long and danger-attended career he had known nothing like this super-crisis which now confronted him.

Angus McPhee hastened on to the held to relieve Joe Tranter of the mascot who had so worthily upheld his high office.

The referee, annoyed intensely at having to deal with such a ridiculous situation, shook himself free of the unfortunate Albion players, and blew his whistle, the ball sailed towards the Albion goal, and the incident was closed.

Extract from the Downside *Football Echo* that evening:

> After the amazing incident recorded above, the Downside players literally took the game into their own hands. Sporting Providence in the queer shape of Neb. had intervened when they stood in dire danger, and they must repay their mascot in kind. That was their mood.
>
> Certain it is that, sturdy as had been the Albion defence up till the dramatic appearance of Nebuchadnezzar, it now crumbled before the determined onslaughts of the home forwards. Tranter claimed the first goal, and in the second half further points were added by Trott and Simister.
>
> The Albion were completely mastered by uncompromising attacks, and these who are inclined to be superstitious may find some ground for faith in the new Downside mascot. The players themselves swear by him – and after to-day's event, who can blame them?
>
> In answer to a question, Mr. McPhee, the new trainer of the Club, made the following statement after the match: "I was holding the goat by the leash when Quinn seemed likely to score. Somehow or other the animal got free."

The pretty girl who met "Happy" Howard by appointment outside *The Echo* office that night knew nothing of the legend which had grown up round Angus McPhee's name in France; but, as she greeted her lover, Nancy Spurgeon was obviously wildly excited.

'Frank!' she cried rapturously; 'what a game! And what a wonderful man that new trainer must be! Did he let that goat loose on purpose?'

'Nancy, my dear, you are asking me to betray State secrets!' replied Howard. 'All I can tell you is that if anyone can save the Downside Club, his name is Angus McPhee. He did the first bit of saving to-day.'

'I'm going to help him, Frank! And *you'll* help him, too, I know, because you're mad on football yourself, although you pretend, being on a newspaper, that you're really above all that sort of thing! tell you what: I'm Going to get *father* to help him as well! Dad was so fed-up the other night that he told me he was going to send in his resignation.

'But,' she continued, with a quick change of tone, 'the bad old days are over now, aren't they, Frank? With the three of us behind him, Mr. What's-his-name will make a good club out of Downside yet – won't he?'

'You bet he will!' replied Howard, emphatically.

CHAPTER VII

McPHEE IS DISCHARGED

Downside had won a match at last! Bankpark Albion had been vanquished. That night the whole town was in a ferment.

Including Mr. Ovens. Not that he shared in the general jubilation; on the contrary. Downside winning that game with the Albion had been the bitterest pill the Club manager could possibly have swallowed. He did not know how to pray, but had he done so, it is almost safe to say that he would have offered up supplication that Downside might sustain the heaviest defeat of its career on this particular afternoon. In that event he could have gone to the directors doubly armed. He could have poured out damning evidence against the new trainer – the man he swore he would "get." Now it would probably take longer, but in any case it was inevitable. He would hound the man out of the town. Thus Horace Ovens in his haste.

He went to the directors at their usual Monday night meeting. He told them that McPhee, the new trainer they had appointed in his absence, and without his sanction, was a desperate character whom they could not trust; that he was letting the team discipline go to blazes; that the incident of the goat had made the Club a laughing-stock for the whole country, and the wrath of the Football Association and the English League authorities would descend upon them inevitably, and that he absolutely refused to work with such a fool. That was straight and that was final; they knew him to be a man of his word and they knew that what he said he meant.

Whereupon Mr. Spurgeon impatiently shifted his eighteen stone of flesh in the vice-chair. 'Let's get down to brass tacks!' he snapped.

'That's what I want to do,' retorted the manager, with some heat. He had net expected this opposition, and it angered him to the point of frenzy. 'Either *he* goes or I do – you can take your choice!' He roared the words out of a flaming face.

'Here, what are you talking about, Ovens?' demanded the chairman. It was not the appalling disaster of losing the services of the individual who had tyrannised over them all so long that made Benjamin Fortey's voice seem strained; it was the tremendous shock which had uprooted him, as it had uprooted everyone else in the room. It was impossible to think of Downside without thinking at the same time of this man who was roaring at them in his wrath.

'What I say!' countered the manager, gaining confidence from the other's tone. 'If you think I'm going to have my authority taken out of my hands by a blasted trainer, and a fellow at that who's blown in from God knows where, and who looks as if he hasn't a clean shirt to his back — a bats-in-the-belfry idiot who's never had any experience of League football before — well, you don't know me! You engaged this fellow when I was away looking for players; you didn't tell me anything about it till it was too late... well, I'm telling you now, if you want to keep him, you won't keep *me* — and your Club can go straight to hell without any interference.'

This was bluff, but the directors had grown so used to being bluffed by Ovens that it had become almost second nature to them.

'The man's only here on a month's trial, Ovens,' said the chairman. This may have been a sop thrown to a bloodthirsty Cerberus, or it may have been merely something to say. In any case, it failed of its purpose.

'Send him going at once,' cried Ovens. 'A fellow like that can do more mischief in a month than I could undo in a year. Get — '

For the second time, Mr. Spurgeon shifted his great bulk impatiently.

'Going to let me go on, Ben?' he asked, looking down the table; and when the chairman, anxious to have his responsibility shifted for the time being, nodded, he turned sharply to the scowling Ovens.

'I don't see as he has done much mischief so far. He won us a match on Saturday, and there wasn't much mischief about that. You always were hot-headed, Ovens; now, straight out, what have you got against the fellow? Has he done anything to you?'

It was at once an unfortunate, and yet a happy question. Horace Ovens had no sense of humour. Had he been more fortunate he would certainly not have answered that shrewd thrust of Spurgeon's.

'Done to me!' he repeated; 'I'll tell you what he did to me. Because I gave him a piece of my mind, he threw me into the plunge-bath in the dressing-room — and I had all my clothes on at the time. He swore it was an accident —'

He couldn't get any further. Mr. Spurgeon was a fat man, and fat men invariably enjoy a laugh. He was soon almost bordering on apoplexy. Even when his fellow directors convinced him of the danger he was running, he shook like a mammoth blanc-mange.

'Ho! ho! ho!' he wheezed. 'Ha! ha! ha!' he rumbled. 'Hell, Ovens! you'll be the death of me.'

'Yes, *damned* funny, ain't it? A waster who nobody knows anything about doing that to *me*... And you laugh your face inside out at it... Right! If that's your answer, I've finished!'

The Downside directors held their breath. If they had obeyed their instinctive feelings, they would have replied to this threat in the only sensible way. They would have told Ovens that the sooner he took his foul tongue out of their office, and his undesirable presence out of the town, the better they would be pleased.

But indebtedness makes cowards of most of us. Besides they had suffered Ovens so long that he had become a habit with them — a bad habit, it was true, but still a habit. The fact was they couldn't visualise the future without Ovens: he had become so inalienably associated with the Club whose mournful destinies they were supposed to control, that their pluck failed them just at the moment when, like a bright star in a murky sky, their deliverance loomed ahead.

'Well, well, there's no need to be so hasty, Horace,' said the chairman, at length. 'We're sensible men, not kids. That certainly wasn't the way for McPhee to behave. We can't have the manager of our Club ducked by a trainer...'

An unholy light gleamed in Ovens' narrow eyes. He knew then he had won.

'If you write out his notice I'll give it him myself in the morning,' he said, jutting out his jaw in the direction of the vice-chairman.

'Agreed, gen'l'men?' asked the chairman, thickly.

'No, Ben — we'll vote on this.' Samuel Spurgeon had awakened to life again.

When the hands were counted — seven for the prosecution, and three for the defence — Samuel Spurgeon rose awkwardly from his elbow-chair, and waddled over to the now smirking manager, whom he tapped on the arm.

'Ovens,' he said slowly, 'I'm taking the liberty of telling you I think you're such a dirty dog that you ought to have a ducking *every* day, and not once a week. That chap McPhee's got to go — but I shall be watching you after this... I'm sixty years of age and eighteen-stone, but holy mackerel, if you touch me, *I'll jump on you!*'

When he thought of the sorry story he would have to tell his daughter, Nancy, the most fervent football follower the Downside Club had ever possessed, when he got home that night, Samuel Spurgeon grew hot with shame.

It was a bright, cold morning. Ovens waited until he had paid all the players, and obtained their receipts, before he handed an envelope to Angus McPhee.

'And that's yours!' he said viciously; 'and when you've read it, and seen that the money's right, the sooner you go the better. That's straight enough, isn't it?'

What was in the envelope was straighter – or more crooked. There was a slip of paper inside a pink slip. The latter was a cheque for £16, and the paper read:

"Dear Sir,

'Recent happenings force the directors to the conclusion that you are unfitted for the post of trainer. Herewith please find cheque for £16, being four weeks' wages at the agreed £4 a week.

The Downside A.F.C.

pp. BENJAMIN FORTEY,

Chairman of Directors."

The inside of him was numbed. He felt as cold as ice. He saw things with an unnatural clearness. It seemed to him that he could look right past those horrible slanting eyes into the evil brain behind.

'You're at the bottom of this, of course,' he said to Ovens, thrusting the envelope into his pocket.

They were standing at the door of the dressing-room, and the clamour behind them of men changing suddenly hushed at the words.

The manager retreated before those questioning grey eyes, but he made no reply.

It was Tommy Trott, the Downside inside-right, who snapped that significant silence.

'Ball practice to-day, McPhee?' he asked.

The discharged trainer turned.

'There's the mon to tell ye that, lads,' he said, motioning towards Ovens; 'it's no' for me to say. I've juist had the sack.'

'I knew it!' exclaimed Trott, as though speaking to himself.

There was another silence after this, broken only by the deep breathing of several men.

Then:

' 'Ell!' said a voice. 'What's the trouble, Mac?'

It was a friendly voice, and it warmed McPhee's cold heart.

'I dinna' ken, lads; I –' he started, when Tommy Trott turned like a revivalist upon his comrades.

'Boys!' he snapped through gritted teeth, 'we know who'll know – Ovens will know! Well ask him, boys – and we'll *make* him tell us, even if he doesn't want to. Mr. Ovens, won't you come inside?'

But Ovens sensed rightly the spirit of that meeting. He preferred to stay outside, where there was no plunge-bath. It was an extraordinary confession for him to make even to himself, but he knew himself in that moment to he afraid of his own players.

'Come *inside*, Mr. Ovens!' called the polite voice again. There was danger in every syllable, and the manager knew it.

He moved away, affecting not to hear. He walked quickly – but not quickly enough. With bewildering rapidity two of the Downside players overtook him; each caught hold of an arm led him back to the dressing-room.

'I'll have you suspended!' he spluttered, but the threat only prompted them to tighten their grip.

The breaking point had definitely been reached by the Downside players. They had suffered so long under this hated taskmaster that it required only the slightest thing to happen to start an explosion.

The trick they knew Ovens must have played them to get rid of the new trainer had been sufficient. The explosion was imminent. Having gone so far, and ventured so much, Trott and his companions were resolved to make the most of this opportunity.

'Lads, this is juist foolishness!'

'The man on whose behalf the insurrection had started knocked up the restraining arms of his would-be champions.

'Mr. Ovens is the manager, lads,' continued McPhee, 'and ye must no' show him disrespect.'

Everyone stared at this; no one quite so fixedly as Ovens himself. But he was a man who cared too much for his own skin to risk having it hurt, and feeling his arms freed, he slunk off while he had the chance.

'Mac,' said Tommy Trott, slowly but impressively, 'you're blasted fool! Here you have lost your job, so you say, through that swine, and when we had him so as we could do what we liked with him, you let him go! What was the sense of that?'

'It would have no mended matters, Tommy,' said McPhee sadly. 'I could have knocked his head off mysel', ye ken, but that would not have done any good.'

There was a silence, an embarrassed silence, and then the inside-right asked: 'Are you going to leave the town, Mac?'

'Aye! 'replied McPhee, wearily. This last reverse threatened to crush him. Nothing lay ahead… and the future had looked fairly bright for him before that tragic morning…

'Well, don't go yet awhile.' With this cryptic rejoinder, Trott turned away.

McPhee moved aside himself. He wanted to be alone; the obvious, and quite unexpected sympathy which the Downside players had shown him, was almost as upsetting as the gloating callousness of Ovens. It showed what might have happened, what might have been done, if he had been given a fair chance.

He must get out of the ground. He would send these good fellows a letter, wishing them good-bye. His feelings were fighting to master him, and if he stayed he might show too clearly what he was suffering.

So he went, while all the Downside players watched from their quarters at the back of the grand-stand.

When he had passed through the big gates, McPhee saw a mammoth human form descend laboriously from a taxi-cab which had just driven up. He recognised the man as Mr. Spurgeon, the vice-chairman of the Club, and, because he felt he could not tolerate speaking to him, he walked rapidly away.

He did not know it, but he had a wrong idea of Samuel Spurgeon.

Back in the dressing-room, the Downside players were heatedly discussing this latest machination of the manager they hated.

The first decent fellow we've had here for years!' said Sam Simister. 'Old Mac was *human*. See what he did over that goat business – and now he's gone!'

'Not yet,' replied Tommy Trott; 'not yet, Sammy boy! Or, if *he* goes, we *all* go! Listen!'

'The better to command his audience's attention, Tommy Trott jumped on to a locker. From this pulpit he preached a rousing gospel. He spoke earnestly, as well as loudly.

Suddenly there came a cheer from the men listening to him.

Covered by the noise, Mr. Spurgeon had been able to creep noiselessly up to the dressing-room door. He heard the remainder of the speaker's remarks.

That he was no ordinary eavesdropper, however, was proved by the rich, expansive smile – a smile of the purest good-humour and transparent honesty – which spread itself over his ample face.

He chuckled softly to himself, and, without spoiling the harmony of the meeting inside the dressing-room, returned the way he had come.

CHAPTER VIII

TOMMY TROTT TAKES A HAND

The telegram had come at six o'clock. After a fourteen miles furious tramp in the country, McPhee had returned to his lodgings wearied in body, but restless in mind. He had formed no plans; the only conclusion he had come to was that he must leave the town.

Where should he go? He grunted. Did it matter where he went? He would pack up his ludicrously few belongings and take the first train for – anywhere.

That decided, he sat down to tea. As he poured out his fourth cup of tea he remembered the telegram. Who had sent it? Had the chairman relented?

He picked up the message, and read it once more.

Call at 42 Grove Road to-night seven.

Without fail. Urgent.

Cramming a twist of tobacco into a blackened briar, he smoked rapidly. The telegram represented a faint hope to him, but he was afraid to put too much faith in it lest it should fail him.

It must be connected in some way with the Downside Club. He remembered the address as that of the chairman. What – ? But speculation was useless; he would get along to 42 Grove Road and solve the puzzle for himself.

When he arrived at the house, some quarter of an hour later, he was told by the maid that Mr. Fortey was in, but that he was engaged.

'Will you please come in and wait,' the girl said.

Even while he was standing at the front door, McPhee heard the sound of voices, apparently in fierce argument. When he took his seat in a small room furnished as a sort of office, he recognised the voice of the speaker as that of Tommy Trott.

What was he doing there? The door had been left slightly ajar, and the words rang out clearly.

'Yes, Mr. Fortey, that's what the boys have told me to tell you – if McPhee goes, we all go! We won't play another game for the Club! If you like to put it in another way, we shall go on strike!'

'You can't know what you're saying, Trott; I'm surprised at a fellow with your common sense talking so through your hat. Why, if you did a thing like that, the Football Association might suspend every man jack of you for a whole year – perhaps for ever! You can't bluff me, my lad!' It was Mr. Fortey who had replied.

Things became clear to McPhee. So this was what Trott had meant when he said that morning, 'Well, don't go yet.' It must have been Trott, also, who had sent him that telegram.

What ought he to do? If it was Trott who had sent that telegram, the chairman of the directors did not know that he was in the house. Ought he to remain?

While he was still debating the point, Trott rallied to the attack.

'Mr. Fortey,' the trainer heard him say, 'do you think any of the fellows playing for the Downside Club at the present time care a damn whether they remain in your team? I don't for one. I've asked you personally time after time to put me on the transfer list, and what have you said: "You can't be spared." It's been the same with Sam Simister, Joe Tranter, and all the rest who are any good. You know that; isn't it the truth I'm telling you?'

'Well!' replied Fortey reluctantly; 'why can't you rest content with Downside? What do you want to go to another club for?'

'Because Downside is a hell that any player who isn't a dog wants to get out of it!' was the reply. 'Why can't you get new players, Mr. Fortey? Why do the boys you've got want to leave? Can you tell me that?'

'*You* seem to know,' was the guarded reply.

'I know! The whole blinkin' world knows! Everyone in football knows! It's because of that swine Ovens! Now *you* know – but if you had eyes in your head, and ears to hear with, you would have known it before!'

'Ah-h!' said a third voice, and by its rumble the listening McPhee knew it to be that of the vice-chairman, Samuel Spurgeon.

'You don't answer, Mr. Fortey!' went on the confident voice of the footballer.

'That's because you know what I'm saying is true! There's Mr. Spurgeon, he knows it's true – knows it as well as I know it!'

'But I've got some more to tell you, Mr. Fortey,' continued Trott – 'and then you can tell me to clear out if you want to. This is what I want to say: Ovens has been the ruin of your team. The boys are all right and, given a chance, can play football. It's Ovens who won't let 'em play! He terrifies the life out of the kids, and the older players don't care. He's a born bully, a foul-mouthed swine, and hangin's too good for him. He's got the mind of a rat!

'Now, listen to something else. We've stood so much, and we won't stand any more. The finish came this morning. This Scotch fellow, McPhee, is a freak, perhaps, but he's human. Besides, he knows his job. We like him – there's no nonsense about him – he's keen, and out to improve the Club. Ovens wants to wreck it. The boys have decided that they want one, but they don't want the other. If they can't have the one they want they'll throw their hand in.'

'And I for one don't blame 'em!' rumbled a voice.

'*Sam!*'

'You needn't "Sam" me, Ben, if you ain't going to use the common sense the Lord gave you!' replied Samuel Spurgeon instantly; 'you've known my opinion of this McPhee business all along. It was dirty, Ben, and we ought not to have soiled our hands with it. If Ovens wants to leave, for the love of Mike let him go – he's the curse of the – !' He broke off suddenly. In his heat the vice-chairman had forgotten that Trott was present.

'Anyhow,' said Trott, with the air of a man playing his last card, 'the players don't think that Mac has been treated right – and if Ovens shows himself on the ground again he'll go off in an ambulance. He's had several warnings. McPhee's got to stay, Mr. Fortey – that's what the boys have told me to tell you I'

'You'd better go into the other room for a few minutes,' replied Fortey.

Trott turned instantly, and a moment later was shaking McPhee vigorously by the hand.

'Have you heard anything?' he asked.

'Iverythin'!' was the succinct reply; 'and I can't possibly –'

'Don't try!' cut in the forward. 'Time enough for that when it's all settled. But we aren't all rotters in Downside.'

Five minutes or so went by, and then Mr. Fortey put his head round the side of the door. His eyes opened ludicrously as he caught sight of the trainer he had given word to be dismissed that morning.

'What–?'

'It's quite all right, Mr. Fortey,' said Trott, promptly. 'I took the liberty of asking Mr. McPhee to call here to-night. I thought it likely that you would want him to sign a contract, or something... We all like Mac as a trainer, Mr. Fortey,' he added, as though as an after-thought. 'And I may tell you that the boys have taken this action through me without McPhee knowing anything about it. As a matter of fact, it was he who stopped us this morning from giving Ovens a damned good hiding.'

'Come in here, McPhee,' said the chairman.

'If you care to sign it – there's a six months' contract on that table,' he went on; 'I suppose it's too late to make apologies and that sort of thing, but if it's any satisfaction to you – I made a mistake this morning. Let it go at that.'

The overshadowing figure of the vice-chairman waddled over to McPhee.

'Sign it!' he said, motioning towards the table; 'I won't let you down.'

Angus McPhee took the pen which Samuel Spurgeon placed in his hand, and wrote his name in the appointed place.

'I think between us we've been a little too hot for Mr. Ovens!' exclaimed the vice-chairman of the Downside Club, and he slapped a massive thigh resoundingly.

Now he could go home and meet the questioning gaze of his daughter, Nancy, without being uncomfortable. As a matter of fact, he was feeling quite jovial, and had already decided to take Nancy to the pictures on the morrow. Nancy loved the pictures.

CHAPTER IX

THE CAMPAIGN COMMENCES

The rout was complete! Horse, foot and artillery had surrendered, and the enemy was in full retreat.

Horace Ovens was a sadly disillusioned man. He had over-estimated his own power, and under-estimated that of the enemy.

Continuing the metaphor, he had retired in confusion, and this confusion increased as the days went by. In an indirect way he had intimated to several other clubs that he might be disposed to consider a change. The answers he received to these "feelers" disconcerted him. Not only did the clubs to whom he had written reply that they could not utilise his services, but they all expressed more or less alarm that he should even have thought of joining their forces. These sentiments were couched in different terms, varying from the brutally frank to the caustically sarcastic, but the same firm "No, thank you!" was plainly to be read in every reply.

McPhee did not know of these letters. Now that the danger had been passed, he was too busy thinking about his job, looking at it from every angle, to worry over his routed enemy. The night that Samuel Spurgeon openly came over to his side, he had a long talk with the vice-chairman, and it had amply compensated him for what he had suffered.

'I may be fat,' Mr. Spurgeon said; 'but I ain't a fool. I don't mind telling you, McPhee, that when I first saw you I thought you were a fool – either that, or stark, staring mad. But I've changed my opinion. I've been keeping my ears and eyes open. If there's one fellow on the face of the earth who can keep this Club above water, I reckon it's you. Anyway, I'm betting on you, and when you want any backing, come to me. I don't say it because you're cheap at four pounds a week. If you make good – and, as I say, I'm both backing and betting on you – I'll see that you get what's owed to you. Ovens ain't going to end his days with Downside – not unless he drops dead without much warning. Take your coat off to it, Scottie!'

That was just what McPhee did. His contract stated that so far as the condition and work of the players was concerned, he was in sole control. That made him coach as well as trainer – and it was more as coach than actually as trainer than he intended to act.

He was met more than half-way in this respect. The Downside players had been actuated to a great extent in their recent sensational action by their hatred of the manager, but Tommy Trott's words in the interview at the chairman's house had been caused by something more than mere hatred of one man – they had contained a tone of respect and admiration for another.

McPhee expressed his thanks for what they had done in a few, brief, bitten-off words that were so charged with the emotion he felt, and were so deeply Scottish, that only a few in the dressing-room really understood what he was saying.

'Now ye'll start to learn football,' he said in conclusion. Everybody understood that all right, for Mac had the inevitable practice ball in his hands at the time.

'Get into your things – quickly,' came the second command, and the players – before so listless, so indifferent, and so inclined to curse themselves only less thoroughly than their surroundings – turned eagerly to their lockers.

This man interested them.

During the next few days strange stories were in circulation. One was that football matches were to be seen *free* on the Downside ground each morning; another that the Downside forwards could be seen playing the fool with a lot of sticks stuck in the ground; another that young Daly did nothing but practise taking corner-kicks for half-an-hour at a time. There was a fourth that some of the "kids" who had joined the team, were smashing each other's faces in owing to the rivalry which existed between them.

These were sensational rumours, and to get further information, many anxious searchers after truth sauntered to the Downside ground; some sauntered, others – such is the quickening fever of football – ran.

But they returned empty; a new system was in operation, they learned. The gates were barred to casual callers. Only those who had legitimate business to transact were admitted to the Downside ground on ordinary occasions.

Baulked in this respect, the students of sensation turned to their newspapers, and these only served to heighten the general interest.

Readers of the *Evening Echo* learned that "the ill-fated Downside F.C. is undergoing a thorough overhauling, so far as the playing strength is concerned. This is all to the good. The present team could not possibly display much worse form than it has done so far this season – but the possibility is that it might be made to play a great deal better. We stake what little personal reputation we may have that the right man is undertaking this overhauling job. The results should soon be seen. In the meanwhile, as a certain contemporary has seen fit to sneer at a man who is working hard for the pure love of sport in our city, we may remark that some people can accomplish more in five minutes than others can in five years – and do it better!"

Although public interest in the doings of Downside had greatly diminished, current events were doing much to revive that interest. First, there had been the startling episode of Neb, the club mascot, doing a goat-ly deed to earn its keep; then had come the mysterious rumours about the new trainer's doings; finally, there was the highly-meritorious draw which Downside effected on the Albion ground in the replay on the following Saturday.

The Sunday papers referred in flattering terms to the "understanding that existed between the two visiting backs and the goalkeeper."

Downside people stared at this. Up till then all departments of the team had been weak, but the weakest section of all undoubtedly was the defence. Between them, Camp, the goal-keeper, and Giles and Gerrish, the two backs, had conceded no fewer than thirty-three goals – and this with the season not half-way run! Although each back was a powerful kick, and a robust, if crude, tackler, the pair had not yet fallen into each other's ways (both were newcomers to the team at the beginning of the season), and the result had been chaos – goals – for their opponents. They had never developed an understanding either between themselves, or with the goalkeeper behind them, who, in consequence, hated them with a dire and dreadful hate. For all their impressive physique (Giles in football uniform looked something like Zbysco[2] the wrestler, when in his prime) they had proved reeds, and Walter Camp, the victim of a malicious fate, would long since have asked for his transfer papers if he had not known that the services of the man who had let more balls go past him than any other goalkeeper in the three Leagues that season were not likely to be in tremendous demand "… good understanding…" It was strange.

In order to see what had happened, another large crowd turned up to see the next home match – against Wovington Wanderers. What was more – the average football enthusiast being the most mercurial person on earth – for the first time since the opening match of the season (when all fond fancies were remorselessly murdered) a note of hope, almost of

____

[2] Stanislau Zbyszko was the ring name of an 18 stone, Polish three-time world heavyweight wrestler in the early 1900s.

optimism, was abroad. Had not the team obtained three points out of a possible four in the last two matches?

Neb, who, by a single bound, had rushed into the limelight a fortnight ago, was led round the playing pitch to be greeted with clamorous delight. The crowd had not forgotten the good he had wrought in the last home match. Perhaps they were hoping –

But the Wanderers were seeing to that. The chairman of the Wovington directors had expressed to the Downside officials a comprehensive opinion of goats in general. He had wound up with the following words:

'Mind you, I'm not saying it wasn't clever – but you can't pull a trick like that off twice. It worked with Bankpark Albion, but you can bet your last collar-stud that it won't work with Wovington Wanderers. We come from a town where there's more wrong 'uns to the square foot than any other place in England. But, mind you, it was clever...' And still mumbling, the man who had given the warning took himself off.

'McPhee,' said Mr. Fortey, going straight into the home dressing-room, 'keep that darned goat well under control to-day. The Wanderers are a tough crowd, and we can't take any chances. If that goat wanders loose, I shouldn't be surprised if he didn't get shot.'

What the woman novelist calls "a wintry smile" played round the lean mouth of Trainer McPhee.

'Neb is too much of an artist to repeat himself,' he said dryly, and went on with his job.

He did not add that the club had received a letter from the Football Association, which Mr. Spurgeon had suppressed, stating that the presence of goats couldn't be permitted inside the playing area once a match had started.

So Neb, within his flannel mascot's jacket, withdrew. He wrought no magic that day. He had come before the crowd, bowed his acknowledgments in answer to the popular acclaim, and gone back to the store-room to eat his dinner. Neb was "resting."

But if Neb did not provide another sensation, the team on whose behalf he worked his mascotry did. Not such a breathless, amazing, heart-stopping sensation as that staged a fortnight ago on the same ground, but still a distinct shock. A pleasant shock, be it added.

Downside had formerly been a team without method. Eleven men garbed for the game had gone out and kicked a ball about. That wasn't football, and it never would have been football. There was no understanding between the backs, no cohesion between the halves, and only the most elementary notion of combination amongst the forwards.

After the first ten minutes – during which time the visitors scored, however – the crowd rubbed their eyes. This was not the old Downside. Many of the efforts were still crude, but each player kept more or less in his proper position, while the team for the first time really played as a team, and not as a collection of individuals.

Three weeks before, that early goal – due to a mistake in timing his tackle by Gerrish, the left back – would have meant the complete collapse of the side. Now there seemed to be something animating the team which had been absent before – it had achieved a *morale*.

Particularly was this noticeable after the interval. The score was still 1-0 against Downside, but, ten minutes after play had been resumed, Sam Simister, at right-half, pushed the ball along the ground to Joe Tranter at outside-right. Instead of blazing a trail as he was accustomed to do to the corner flag, Tranter beat his back by cutting inwards. With a virility that none of the spectators suspected the excitable but hitherto back-shy winger of possessing, he forced his way clean up to the penalty line. There he was fiercely tackled by the Wanderers' right back, but before he fell to the turf, he tapped on the ball neatly to his partner, Tommy Trott.

Something had charged the inside-right as it had changed the rest of the team. Hitherto he had always conveyed the impression that he had been induced to come on to this field only by sheer necessity and that the whole business bored him excessively.

Tommy Trott snapped up the pass, tipped the ball to the right with his left foot, swerved past a Wovington half-back who had come rushing back in a frantic effort to retrieve the situation, and then there was that once-deadly right foot swing of his...

"Goal!"

Is there a more heartening cry in the world than that jerked-out word which signifies a football being deftly driven home? Certainly there is no word in our language into which is packed so much fierce joy, so much triumphant exultation, and so much strident challenge. It is the very flesh and blood of the game.

The Downside crowd did not realise what had really happened for some seconds. The shock was almost too much for them. Goals had been very scarce on the Downside ground – except those which caused the opposition to gallop gleefully back to the centre, shaking hands with themselves. It was not until the eager-eyed throng at the back of the Wovington goal had given tongue, that the full import of what Trott had done was appreciated.

Shock followed shock. After the timid Joe Tranter had shown that he possessed courage, and the listless Tommy Trott had demonstrated that he could still get a goal, various other members of the team displayed unexpected gifts.

One weakness of Daly, the young outside-left, whose first season this was in professional football, was his wretched finishing. He was fast and fearless – although only ten stone in weight. He bundled into an opponent in a refreshingly whole-hearted fashion, and took hard knocks with a smile on his freckled face that had endeared him to the crowd.

Up to a point, Daly was good – very good, in fact. But just at the moment when he should have put the seal on his work, when he should have rounded it off – he had a habit of putting the ball lamely outside.

It annoyed the crowd, much as they liked the freckled smiler. If Daly had not been gifted with an obviously easy-going nature, it is possible that the terms the Downside supporters used in conveying their views on the subject would have broken the young outside-left's heart.

But, just as it was a new Trott that the crowd had seen that afternoon, so it was a new Daly. The freckled winger appeared to have found a new left foot. Time after time, even when running at top speed, he put across centres that to a football connoisseur were real works of art. Twice from these ideal crosses, Trott hit the cross-bar, and once Hart, the centre-forward, fired just wide of the upright. The Downside supporters rubbed their eyes – as well they might. There was something almost uncanny about this revival of a moribund team; it was as though a corpse had started to life, waving arms and legs simultaneously.

The greatest eye-opener of all, however, was to come.

When Giles, the right back, hard pressed twenty yards from goal, and with Gerrish, his partner, standing over twelve feet away from him, suddenly turned round, and to the speechless amazement of the crowd, he – *shot straight at his own goalkeeper*!

In that pulsating moment, when men clutched at their collars, and their hearts turned to stone, all life seemed to stand still. The only sign of animation on the face of the universe was Walter Camp, fielding with confident ease the shot that had been fired at him by his own colleague. *He seemed to have expected it!*

Then the explosion came. Pandemonium reigned. What did Giles mean by it? Had he gone mad? Shooting at his own goal… the very thought caused every sell-respecting and proper-thinking head of hair on the ground to bristle.

'I haven't seen that done in English football for over twenty years,' said one man in the stand. 'They knew how to play football in those days. It strikes me,' he continued, 'the fellow who told Giles to sling that ball back to the goalkeeper knows a bit about the game himself.' And smiling a reminiscent smile, he turned once more to the game.

CHAPTER X

DOWNSIDE TRAINS

McPHEE had made a good start; that was important, but he knew that what was infinitely more important was keeping it up. In football, the heroes of to-day are the has-beens of to-morrow. Getting four points out of a possible six (Downside had drawn their home match with Wovington Wanderers, 1-1) was only step. An important one; but still a step.

McPhee had made certain progress, but what had already been accomplished was so little in comparison with what was yet to do. When he was alone, he would sit staring through the heavy smoke from his pipe into a future that was peopled with such strange, and perhaps, impossible fancies, that he dared not share them with anyone – not even with "Happy" Howard, who, with fountain-pen or fist, would have fought till he dropped for the man who was teaching Downside how to play football.

For the present, Ovens was lying low. He was still with the Club, but contented himself with performing his secretarial duties. Although he was always present when the directors met to pick the team, he rarely objected to the men whose names the trainer submitted in writing to the chairman. McPhee realised that this silence was ominous; but he had other matters to think about.

He was pushing his theories, revolutionary as most of them were to the modern football mind, home as hard as he could. To the players who exhibited a painful hesitancy on the field of play he introduced a set of boxing gloves, and ordered them to spar. His experience in the army was that nothing gives a man greater confidence against his fellow man than a few bouts with the gloves. This method had already worked wonders with Joe Tranter, the outside-right.

Each player had been carefully studied, and his weaknesses (in most cases, they were plural) noted. It then became the duty of the trainer to eradicate these defects. The men who were weak in dribbling were made to practise (as that Old Master, Johnny Goodall,[3] practised in his day) dribbling round sticks placed at a distance of a yard apart. Those who were weak in markmanship were forced to practise for hours at a stretch trapping the ball and shooting.

McPhee early found that the best kicker of a dead ball in the whole team was Giles, the right back, and a practice morning never went by without this back taking at least a dozen practice penalty kicks; while at least twice a week half-an-hour's actual playing practice was held, first team forwards against first team defence.

'Football is a trade,' McPhee said after one of these serious bouts, 'and it must be lairnt like any other trade. That's why ye'll keep on practisin'. And keep the ball on the ground more; all the best football is played on the floor. That was what the old Scottish Internationals used to say, and they could have walked through any modern team. And speakin' about team play...'

McPhee would not finish his sentence, but invariably turned to a blackboard that he had rigged up in the dressing-room. Practice and precept were the two words that guided Angus McPhee's existence at this time Every new scheme of play that flashed through his mind he imparted to the Downside players by means of blackboard diagrams, much after the manner of a schoolmaster instructing pupils.

The novelty of the new training fascinated the men at first, and after that the natural desire to shine caused the practice games to be "all-out" affairs from beginning to end. McPhee invariably refereed these pet games of his, and he allowed no slacking.

Much had been done by the time that Christmas drew near. The general air of listlessness that had formerly been the chief characteristic of the Downside camp was gone; the new trainer had swept it away by sheer force of personality. His burning enthusiasm had become contagious; the Downside players had learnt through him to have respect for themselves, if not for the club whose colours they wore. His words had sunk into them.

'Lads,' he had said one morning, when a request made to the directors that a gymnasium be provided had been refused, 'don't let the fact that you're playin' for a poor club affect your game. A man owes it as a duty to himsel' to play his best in every match. No matter how clever a player may be, if he doesna' gi'e his talent a chance, he'll slip doon th' hill. Set yourself a standard – every mon of ye – and try to live up to it.

---

[3] John Goodall was one of the Preston Invincibles of 1888-9 – undefeated the whole season in both League and Cup.

Downside is not mooch of a club the noo, but if it is ever to be made better, and turned into a First Division team again, it's you lads who'll do it – dinna forget that.'

Father, mother and family doctor in one; that was what McPhee became to the Downside Football Club, just as in former days he had been the guide, philosopher and friend of the 5th Scottish Unbendables team.

CHAPTER XI

NANCY ISSUES ORDERS

Christmas had come and gone. McPhee walked with a firmer step. He was more sure of himself. With the passing of the Old Year had gone some of his troubles. Many still remained, but he viewed the future in one sense with something like optimism. The English Cup Competition would soon be starting. Lowly teams had done well in the Cup before now. This was a fascinating form of speculation, but he resolutely put the subject away from him when it became too absorbing. He had to deal with facts, not dreams.

This much could be said, however: Downside was a vastly different team from what it had been in November when he had taken over the training and coaching of the most disappointing side in England. A football club cannot be built in a day, but the ceaseless endeavours that McPhee had made were shown not only in the better position of the Club in the League table – Downside were now fifth from bottom – but also in the immeasurably improved play of the team. Downside had put many of the trainer's imaginations into practice.

The result of this improvement was reflected in the players themselves. They were contented, and while they used to swear at their manager – they did so still whenever they had a chance – they now swore by their trainer. He was the man around whom their present life revolved.

A more hopeful note was shown by the supporters, also. But for the present wave of trade depression, which had swept over that part of the country like a black plague, the attendances would have reached quite respectable figures. Knowing how dependent a football club is on the financial position of the men who form its crowd of supporters, McPhee did not care to look too closely into the future. With regard to the team itself he had hopes – but he knew that the Club was heavily, almost hopelessly, in debt. A bombshell might come at any moment.

It came in the morning of the first home match in January. An eager voice called to him over the Club telephone: 'Seen that about the Club in

The Daily Flash? I hope it's not true; anyway, they didn't get it from me.' It was Happy Howard of *The Echo* speaking, and there was in his voice that which caused McPhee to send out for a copy of the paper in question at once. He was not long in finding the bombshell.

DOWNSIDE'S GRAVE POSITION

We understand that the position of Downside, the club which has shown such an astonishing revival of form lately, is extremely critical. Our information is to the effect that the present directors, harassed by financial worries, will shortly announce that they are not prepared to undertake further financial responsibility. This will probably mean that the famous old club – for don't forget that Downside really *was* a famous club at one time – will have to be wound-up. In any case, the outlook cannot be said to he anything but extremely critical.

It is significant that several First Division managers are reported as having announced their intention of being present at Downside to-day when the ill-fated club are due to play Willsbridge Town.

Even the Scot's habitual stoicism could not prevent him from showing the effects of such a blow. It was almost a knock-out. Of course, the story might be a canard, but he felt convinced that there was truth in it. Mr. Spurgeon had told him that the directors owed no less than £9,000 on the ground alone. They had bought the enclosure during the war because it was a case of either buying it or clearing out, which would have meant the end of the Club. It was thought then that they had done a shrewd stroke of business, but now –

He folded the newspaper and carefully put it in his overcoat pocket. If others had seen that article, and no doubt they had, so much the worse, but they would not hear the news from him. He did not want his players upset. Whether the Club smashed or not, the duty of everyone for the moment was to win the game that day with Willsbridge Town. That was how he saw it.

The players came trooping in now to their light luncheon. One of the innovations McPhee had made was to have the players lunch together on the ground before each home match. He could tell by their faces that they knew the dread tidings and were eagerly discussing the matter. Yet none inquired his opinion. This seemed to him rot only strange, but callous, until he remembered how, in a former crisis, these same men, or the

49

majority of them, had shown him such splendid loyalty. Perhaps it was because the Downside players had the same kindly regard for his feelings that they did not come to him now.

As he had promised himself, no word came from him, and when he approached a group to fit them for action, all conversation ceased. The players were evidently determined that the subject, which was of absorbing interest to all of them, should not be discussed in front of the trainer, or even in his hearing. McPhee was content; he had no heart for such a talk with its myriad by-paths of gloom and speculation.

'Guid luck, lads!'

It was with these words that McPhee had always sent his team out to battle since he had been the Downside trainer. He tried to keep his voice steady, and he believed he had done so, but Tommy Trott turned and went back.

'Mac, old man – ' he started; then, finding the words would not come so easily as he had imagined, he turned and rushed after his comrades. It was an eloquent action, and McPhee knew that Trott would not only play a particularly hard game himself that day, but would induce the rest of the team to do so.

In the course of time, the trainer took himself out to the long bench by the white railings below the grand-stand, which was his seat of office when a match was on, and once again gazed at the scene which had become so familiar – so dearly familiar – to him.

He felt something gripping him. All his hopes were centred on that patch of churned turf, with the white goal-posts standing sentinel at either end. It was here he had laboured, putting not only all his physical but his mental strength into the job. If he were banished now from that open-air workshop of his, it would be infinitely harder than it had been a few weeks back. Then he had only *intended* to do – now he had actually *done* it – not half, nor yet a quarter of what he hoped, but still something, a great deal even, considering the time.

He knew, his commonsense told him, that he had done good work. Take Joe Tranter, for instance, the outside-right, who was now fretting on the touch-line, waiting for the pass which seemed so long in coming. He had made Tranter a great winger. He had first cured him of his fatal hesitancy, and then, when this boy with the volatile temperament had threatened to go to the other extreme, he had toned him down. There was also the occasion when he had taught him the lesson that each man is born to his particular job, and that he is a fool if he attempts something for which he is totally unfitted, and which is quite out of his line.

'Come along, you bonny boys!'

The challenging, glorying words reached him from the towering grand stand behind. They were cried by a man carried away by the magic of the game, the glamour of the purposeful raid which the home forwards looked like scheming to a successful end.

The ball could be seen going from man to man. Trott, the inside-right, had it now. Taking in the situation at a glance he bewildered the Willsbridge defence by booting it clear across the field to Daly, when the obvious move would have been to feed his own partner, Tranter, who seemed admirably placed.

But Downside were not playing obvious football these days. They had received almost daily instruction from a man who saw into the finer points of the game as into a mirror; a man who had a wonderful natural gift for the scientific side of the people's pastime, who saw in every match a battle of strategy as well as of physical force and skill; a man who moved his footballers in those mimic matches he played on the blackboard in the dressing-room much as a skilled chess player moves his pieces.

So Trott had sent that disconcerting long pass clean across the field…

Daly trapped the ball, feinted to go on, and then cut inwards. Prancing like a colt, he fooled two defenders and then, making believe to shoot, focused the attention of the remaining bock upon himself. In a flash the outside-left sent an ideal pass to the waiting centre-forward, who, rushing on with terrific speed, caught the ball as it dropped on his right instep.

A flash, an outstretched arm, a roar – and Downside had scored the opening goal! The foot was the foot of Hart, but the brain was that of Angus McPhee. That goal had been obtained by following out some of the moves the trainer had made on his instructional blackboard.

The cheers that greeted the scoring rang out as a sort of challenge. Who said Downside were down and out? Who said they couldn't play football? The worst team in England, were they? – well, that goal would show them! From the grand-stand there came a hysterical, cracked bellow –

'*Why, you're a real team!*'

There was a laugh at this; for why not? Willsbridge, one of the strongest sides in the Second Division, had had their defence overrun by a forward line that a few weeks before had been impotent. The crowd were in a mellow mood, when all life seemed melodious. Give any football crowd an early goal by the home side, and you will see human nature at its merriest, and best. Good humour bubbles from it.

If McPhee had not seen the devastating news in *The Daily Flash* that day he, in his dour, grim, yet very sufficient way, would have responded to the mood of the delighted crowd. Mentally he would have danced with them. Now –

Somewhere up in the stand, watching keenly, critically, appraisingly, were representatives of some of the greatest clubs in the land. Hungry hawks, these men, who would snatch any player they favoured without scruple or compunction. McPhee had trained, had educated, had "made" many of these Downside players, and now they would shortly be bid for like geese at a Christmas fair…

And it would not be mere flesh and blood, nimble feet and lithe, well-trained muscular bodies that would be concerned in the selling; no, his labour, his brain, and his hopes would go with them. He did not mind the first two so much, but who would give him back his hopes when the players who embodied them were gone? True, there was the letter… but that would not be the same.

He had no more time for further musing from now on to the interval, for the game waxed fast and furious, and he had plenty to do seeing to knocked-out and otherwise injured players.

During the five minutes interval, also, he was too busy with his hands to b a able to think about anything except the job in hand. It was not until eight o'clock that night when he sat before a fire in his lodgings that he really settled down to try to think out the position which he was convinced he would shortly have to meet.

There was a hurried knock at the door, and *The Evening Echo* reporter, Howard, burst into the room. For once he belied his nickname of "Happy."

'I've got it out of Fortey over the 'phone,' he said excitedly. 'Tranter, Trott, Daly, Hart and Simister on the transfer list! Middlebridge want the right wing. Hilltown Athletic are after Daly – and they'll take Hart, too, if the price isn't too high – and Summerhill have set their hearts on Simister! Talk about the slaughter of the Innocents What a clearance sale… ! Can't stop a moment now; I just dropped in to tell you, but must cut along to the office now to see that the news gets into the Stop Press. My hat! but this is the sensation of the season… ! Back in a few minutes if you feel like talking about it.'

McPhee shifted uneasily in his chair. That afternoon the team he had lifted out of the mud, the team he had taught to play football, had whipped one of the strongest sides in the Second Division 2-0. And now these men – the very cream of them – were being taken away from him. At the best he would have to start afresh; at the worst, there would be no Downside Club left, and he would be cumbering the earth…

Another knock on the door broke in upon his reverie. A series of wheezes preceded the enormous bulk of Mr. Samuel Spurgeon.

'Come in to have a bit of a chat, McPhee,' he said, gingerly lowering himself into a decrepit-looking arm-chair that has thousands of relations in "furnished apartments for respectable young gentlemen" all over the country.

'It's a bad job,' went on the vice-chairman; 'that's why I came along to have a talk with you. Downside to-day is what you've made it – I know that, and that's why I've come. Want to ask any questions?'

McPhee roused himself, stuffed black tobacco into a blacker pipe, and turned to his visitor.

'I juist want to ken the truth,' he said, grimly.

'That's the only thing worth knowing. It's like this: At the present time goodness only knows what is to become of the Club.

'It's touch and go. Now, don't blame the directors, as everyone else will do once it's public property – as it will be before many minutes are passed. In a nutshell, Downside is so heavily in debt that it can't go on.

'The fact is that the present Board won't agree to carry on the Club any longer under the present conditions – it doesn't feel justified in doing so. We were badly in the cart before the war. Then we were forced to buy the ground, and had to borrow heavily to do it. The bank, as well as other creditors agreed that our debts should remain in abeyance (so long as the interest was paid, of course) until our luck began to change. As you know – for you've been with the Club long enough now to know all about us – our luck went from bad to worse; we could do nothing right. You and I know what was the chief cause of it all, but there were other reasons as well. It's not for me to run down the men who sit on the board with me, and I'm not going to do so – but, well, perhaps I had better not say anything more.

'Anyway, this is the rotten position to-day: Our creditors are now demanding immediate payment. To put it in a nutshell once more, these creditors can't see any hope for us. Besides, they want their money. There you've got it! What do you think about it?'

'The Cup Ties will soon be here.' McPhee could not help shifting in his seat again.

'Granted. But we owe barrels of money, son! Just think – £9,000 on the ground alone… Still, it's a hell of a pity!'

'How many men are ye – sellin'?' McPhee baulked over the last word.

'All of 'em any good! That's the only way out – you must see that for yourself. We've had several offers already; but the final decisions will be made at the board meeting on Monday night. You'll be there, of course?'

'I suppose so.' The bitterness he felt was reflected in his face.

Samuel Spurgeon rose with difficulty from the chair he had

practically ruined. He looked at McPhee's grim face, and crossed over to the man.

'It's hellish bad luck: I'll say that!' he mumbled. 'When this bombshell came, the first fellow I thought of was you – and that's the Gospel truth… well… I must be getting along.'

The man who had endeavoured to give the stricken trainer of the Downside Club what solace was possible, was met at his front door by his daughter, whose lightest whim was generally law with him.

'Father,' she said, 'I want to speak to you.'

'Oh – ah!' Mr. Spurgeon knew what that determined tone meant.

Feeling uncomfortable, for Nancy Spurgeon generally prefaced a lecture with these words, he allowed himself to be drawn into the living-room, and dumped down in his chair.

'Put your pipe on – you great big baby! I know it's no good talking to you unless you're smoking.'

Obediently the vice-chairman of the Downside Football Club drew his pipe and tobacco from his pocket.

'Daddy!'

The sharply uttered word forced him to look up. He saw the girl who was everything in the world to him wagging a slim finger at him in admonition. Nancy Spurgeon, had she but known it, never looked a more bewitching captor of men's hearts than she did at that moment.

'Daddy!' she said again, 'what are you going to do about the Downside Club?' Her tone suggested eager curiosity and suppressed excitement.

'What *can* I do?' replied her father. 'There isn't one chance in a thousand of the Club being allowed to live. Everything's against it –'

'Then *make* it live!' cried the girl, on tip-toe now with excitement, her voice vibrant with enthusiasm. 'Daddy! If you stand by and let that Club die, I shall never forgive you!'

'God bless my soul!' ejaculated Samuel Spurgeon. 'What can I do? haven't got thousands of pounds, and if I had, I should have more sense than to invest it in a professional football club – especially a club like Downside. No, my dear, I've lost enough already. Of course,' seeing the look of dismay on his daughter's pretty face, 'if there was even a sporting chance –'

'There *is*! There *is*! Listen, father! Remember what that new trainer – you know, the man with the Scotch face and the funny name, McPhee, isn't it? – has done already! Why, it's a different team! And if he can do that in a few weeks, what can he do by the end of the season?'

'There's nobody in this town more likely to remember what McPhee's done than I am, Nan. But even he isn't a magician. Don't you see that if all the best players are sold – as they will have to be sold to pay of the chief debts of the Club--he'll have nothing left to build up the team with. No, my dear, I'm sorry – but there's absolutely no help for it. I wish I had resigned some weeks ago, as I intended, because I must say I don't like the job which has cot to be done on Monday night.'

'Daddy, I feel sure there must be some way! And… and can't you see that it will affect Frank? He follows the Downside team – if there's no Downside to write about, he may – may lose his job! And then he would have to leave the town, and then – then – '

'Then there would be a certain young lady whose name I needn't mention who would be going about with red eyelids, eh? You know, my young minx, that you never really consulted me about going out with young Howard. He's a decent enough young chap; I'm not going to say he isn't; but –'

'Oh, I know what you are going to say, Daddy. He doesn't make enough money for us to get married on. But he will – that is, if you are plucky enough to save the Downside Club. You see, if the Club is saved, and gets back into the First Division, or does well in the Cup, Frank will not only get a better job on *The Echo*, but he will also make a lot of money writing about Downside football in other papers. I've been thinking it all out.'

'So it seems,' chuckled her father.

'Not that I want to be selfish about it, Daddy: because it will benefit Frank is not the only reason why I don't want the Downside Club to die. You know how I love to watch the team play, even when it does badly. You know that it's the one great interest I've got – outside of you – and Frank. Daddy, can't you stop them winding-up the Club on Monday night?'

Soft, rounded arms were about Samuel Spurgeon's neck; rose-leaf lips were pressed against his scrubby left cheek.

'Think – Daddy!' commanded Nancy Spurgeon. The vice-chairman of the Downside Club puckered his brow for several seconds, and then jumped unsteadily to his feet.

'Sink me! I'll try it!' he said.

CHAPTER XII

MR. SPURGEON DECLARES WAR – AND THEN PLAYS HIS LAST CARD

'We'll get to business!' said the chairman. There was a sudden craning forward. This was a big, a critical, moment in the life of the Downside F. C, and all except the man who was feeling the situation the most acutely openly portrayed their expectancy. Their faces were open books. The one exception sat in the far corner, smoking his eternal black pipe. He looked stolidly in front of him.

'Gentlemen,' said the chairman, looking straight ahead and not at the faces of the men he was addressing, 'you all know that this is perhaps the most momentous meeting in the history of the Downside Football Club. It may well be the last meeting we shall hold in this board room.

'There is no one more sorry to have to say this than I am myself, but, gentlemen, facts are facts, and facts have to be faced. It is no use our blinking at them. The plain truth is that we find ourselves unable to carry on. We are all business men as well as sportsmen, and, being business men, we know that we should be exceedingly foolish to allow any sentiment we might have to go against our common sense. It is our common sense which tells us now to clear out as soon as possible –'

'That's straight enough, anyway,' broke in a voice.

'Straight enough,' repeated the chairman, still looking straight in front of him, as though he were speaking to an imaginary audience instead of to a real one. 'Yes, it's my intention to speak straight to-night – facts have to be faced, as I said before. Any man who doesn't speak straight to-night would be a damned fool!'

'That's right!'

One man said it, and at least four others supported him.

'It's bad luck, as I said before, but apparently this Club hasn't a dog's chance to keep on. That means it must die. The people to whom we owe money have practically decided that it must die by suddenly demanding

"

that we pay our bills without any more delay. Now we all know, gentlemen, that they have been very patient with us, the bank especially, but everyone has a limit, and now these men have decided that they have reached theirs. Personally, I can't honestly say I blame them!'

The speaker paused as if expecting to receive some criticism at this point, but none came. Each man seemed busy with his own thoughts.

'If there was any hope I wouldn't mind going on,' continued Mr. Fortey, 'but there isn't! This trade depression has put the last nail in our coffin, and the best thing we can do is to clear out – *now!* He brought his right fist down with a crash on to the table in front of him.

It was a significant gesture, and if there had been any wavering on the part of the other directors it would, no doubt, have had a considerable effect. But, apparently, the speaker had been carrying his audience with him right from the start.

'That's right' repeated the man who had spoken before, and again there was a ready assent from all round the long table except the bottom where the vice-chairman, Mr. Samuel Spurgeon, was busily engaged in the childish business of playing a game of noughts and crosses with himself.

'I say *now!* continued the chairman, 'because the first bit of luck that's come our way – since I joined the board, anyway – happened to-day.'

Picking up a piece of paper, the speaker continued: 'As you know, gentlemen, there were present at the game on Saturday representatives from several First Division teams. They seemed struck with the play of some of our players – fortunately for us – because the money we shall receive through the transfers of these men will be a godsend to us.'

'Let's have the list, Ben.'

The chairman responded to the appeal by reading from the paper he held in his hand.

'Middlebridge want Joe Tranter and Trott, and they are willing to pay £3,500 for the pair of 'em – you can bet I stuck the price on as much as I could; then Hilltown want young Steve Daly – £2,000 is the price I fixed on Daly, for he's a good kid, and he's playing real good football lately. They'll also take Hart if the price is reasonable. Hart has been showing much improved form at centre-forward during the last few matches, as you know, gentlemen. What shall we say – £1,000?'

'£1,500,'came an eager seconder.

'Well, £1,500 then – we can always climb down a bit. Then there's Sam Simister. Summershill are willing to go high for Sam. I've put him down at £1,500. Altogether, gentlemen, there'll be a nice little sum of £8,500 or so coming in over the transfer of these players. Our share of that will clear off all our outstanding debts with the exception of what we owe the bank. The bank will be on the safe side because they've got the deeds, and the ground is worth a darned sight – don't we know it – more than £9,000 to anybody.'

'Why not keep it ourselves, then?'

Sam Spurgeon had ceased playing noughts and crosses with himself on the writing-pad before him to ask this pertinent question.

The chairman looked down the long table, it seemed regretfully, while when he replied he used a tone of mild reproach.

'Sam,' he said, 'you've always had the reputation of being a businessman!'

There was no rancour in the words, but the effect was the same as though Spurgeon had been smacked across the face. With startling unexpectedness he rose from his seat, sending the heavy chair spinning away from him. His usually good-natured face was flushed with anger, and when the words came they raked the room.

'Yes, Ben Fortey, I've always been known as a business man, and I've always flattered myself that I am a business man. But by God! I couldn't do the business that you've just transacted – not in the damnably cold-blooded way you've done it, anyhow!

'I'm still vice-chairman of this Club, and I intend to speak my mind,' continued Spurgeon, his determined voice rising high above the angry clamour which his opening sensational words had called forth from the majority of his fellow directors. 'And this is what I'll tell you to your faces, and be damned to you! – You're a lot of white-livered skunks, and I snap my fingers at the whole lot of you!' He did so with a gesture of infinite, overwhelming contempt.

'I'm a business man right enough,' he continued, glaring round, 'and there's no one in this room who has more cause to regret the heavy debts that the Club has piled up than myself, since there is only the chairman who has committed himself for the same amount of financial responsibility. But do you know what you reminded me of when you were fixing those prices on your players just now? A lot of butchers selling sheep!

'You needn't waste your breath by growling at me. And you needn't run away with the idea that because I'm fat I'm also a soft-hearted fool. I know that the only way for us to clear off the best part of the debts is to raise the money by selling the best players. Any club would do it. That isn't my point – '

'What is your point?' A man half-way down the table on the left-hand side glared at him in turn.

'*This!*' The word was hurled like a weapon. 'You talked of getting rid of the men who have been doing their best for the Club, who really had the welfare of Downside at heart, as though – as though, as I said before, they were so much cattle. There was never a word said about any of you being sorry – ugh! you make me feel sick…

'But I could have forgiven even that if you had said a single word about the man in this room to whom you will owe practically every penny that you will get for the transfer of the Downside players. Yes, you can stare, but what was the value of the whole rotten team before McPhee – yes, he's the man I mean – carne? Why, I wouldn't have given £1,000 for the whole of the first side! And now you're calmly talking about getting £8,500 for less than half of the team – and never a word to the man to whom you owe the money!

'Who was it turned these duds into real players? McPhee! Who has done more for Downside, and worked harder than any other man connected with the Club during the past few weeks? McPhee! Who brought the value of the players to be sold from practically nothing to the wonderful sums you are asking for them to-day? McPhee! Do you admit it! Do you tell him that you are sorry that all his splendid work as a trainer has gone for nothing so far as he is concerned? You do not! Did you even tell him of this sudden crisis which has arisen? You did not! He only knew about it through reading the news in a London morning paper. Who sent that information to London? That's what I want to know. Perhaps you can tell me, Ovens?' And he swirled round in the direction of the Downside manager, who had been regarding him angrily ever since he had got on his feet to speak.

'Well, suppose I could? Suppose I gave the news out myself? What about it?' Ovens was openly truculent, so confident, indeed, that he must have felt he had the majority of the meeting behind him.

'Then I say – and I don't care whether a single man in this room agrees with me or not – that you were a traitor to your own Club, Ovens! I always felt that you couldn't be trusted, and now I know you can't!'

'What your opinion is doesn't matter a rotten orange, Spurgeon!' Horace Ovens, instead of ignoring the insult, actually seemed to welcome it. He sprang forward, looking almost ludicrous in his exhibition of rage. 'Quite the loving stepfather, ain't you?' he sneered; 'kicking up this fuss because that fool,' pointing to McPhee, who was leaning forward himself by this time, 'talked you round to his damned rot! You have always been on his side. Yes, it was me who suggested to the chairman that the clubs we knew were out to buy players should be told exactly how Downside stood at the present time. We knew they would send scouts down for the game with Willsbridge Town, and that it would be a sort of Leeds City auction[4] all over again. I did that for the good of the Club,' continued the manager, challengingly.

'Mind my split lip!' snorted the vice-chairman in scathing contempt. 'You did it because you were afraid you wouldn't get your wages to the end of the season unless some money was got from somewhere – that's why you did it. But you're finished, Ovens – you're finished, I tell you!'

'Finished! We're all finished! The damned Club is finished, isn't it? What are you so sore about – because your pal has lost his job and won't ever stand a chance of getting another?'

There were many sensations that night, but the greatest was to come.

'Downside's finished, is it?' stormed Samuel Spurgeon. 'Then let me tell you all that the Club is not finished. That's another time you've been wrong, Ovens! Sell what players you like, Ben Fortey, and after you've sold 'em, and pocketed the money, leave Downside to me! I'll take over the rest of the debts along with the boys who are left – and McPhee! I thought you were a straight dealer, Fortey, but I find you're not. You've worked hand in hand with Ovens, and all the rest of you have agreed with the dirty business. Well, have no more to do with any of you. I hope you don't want it straighter than that, but if you do, you can have it.' He paused, glaring up and down the long table. Men were clenching their fists and grinding their teeth. The shock had taken their breath away.

'You may think that I'm a fool, but I tell you that Downside isn't going to be allowed to die. The Club will be carried on – and you,' suddenly wheeling and pointing a quivering finger at Ovens, 'won't be the manager of it – I'll take damned good care of that! McPhee will be the manager – McPhee, the man none of you have thrown a decent word to since he came here, but who has put about £6,000 in your pockets in as many weeks. McPhee, who could have gone to the Swifts as a football adviser, but who stayed on with this hell of a Club because he was a man, and not an apology for one!' As though he was compelled to do so, the speaker turned once more in the direction of Ovens.

There was a moment's silence. The information which Spurgeon had hurled at the meeting was too flabbergasting for immediate comment. Then, like a pack of jackals, they started to howl. Ovens was the first to find his tongue.

'Bah! You're crazy!' he cried. 'The only use the Swifts could have for a fellow like McPhee would be to push the heavy roller up and down!'

'Mac!'

---

[4] Leeds City were formed in 1904 and were expelled from the League in 1919 for dodgy dealings and the directors refusing to co-operate with the FA inquiry; following this an auction of the players was held at a Leeds hotel.

Samuel Spurgeon looked across at the trainer. 'Do you mind lending me that letter for a minute?'

McPhee came awkwardly forward. That letter was his secret, and he did not know how Spurgeon had come to learn about it. In any ordinary circumstances he would have refused the request – but now his spirit leapt to that of this staunch and selfless sportsman.

'This letter was written to McPhee a fortnight ago,' said Spurgeon, holding an envelope in his pudgy fingers. 'I only heard of it through one of the Swifts' directors, who sent me a private letter this morning. McPhee himself told no one. When I spoke to him about it just before this meeting, he said he didn't want to discuss it. But I made him – if no one else knows, *I* know what he has done for Downside in a few weeks, and I am going to take care that he gets the credit for it. This is what the Swifts wrote to him a fortnight ago:

> "Dear Sir,
>
> "A representative of this Club has been in Downside lately, and has conveyed such information to us about yourself that, if at any time you should feel inclined for a change, we should be pleased to give you an opportunity of developing your undoubted ability as a football coach with our Club.
>
> "Yours faithfully,
> "For the Swifts A.F.C.,
> "A. T. GURNEY,
> "Secretary.

'The most scientific club in England; not only the runners-up in the First Division, but the winners of the English Cup last year! – the Swifts want what you would have chucked away 'Sell your players; McPhee's going to stick by me, and between us we'll get some new ones!'

Having played the last card, Samuel Spurgeon walked to the door. He was followed by McPhee.

Had anyone spoken to the trainer of the Downside Football Club during the next thirty seconds, he would have been astonished at the sight of a strong man bursting into tears.

CHAPTER XIII

CUP-TEAM RECRUITING

When Mr. Spurgeon arrived at the meeting which was to decide the fate of the Downside Football Club he had no intention of making any foolhardy heroic stand against the force of circumstances. Financially he could not afford it. When he had said the cryptic words, 'Sink me. I'll try it!' in the presence of his daughter on the previous Saturday evening, he meant that he would plead with his fellow directors to run the team for the rest of the season, hoping against hope that the experiment would justify itself.

But while listening to the cold-blooded bargainings of Mr. Fortey he had "found" himself – spiritually. Deep down in his nature was an emotional side. He had never suspected it before that night – certainly not in a football sense. Something had, however, called it forth, and when he hoisted himself to his feet it was in full flood. Mr. Spurgeon rose to astonishing heights in a very short space of time.

Talking is not of much use to some men; they want "showing." Angus McPhee had shown the vice-chairman of the Downside F.C. what enthusiasm and love for a man's job can do. Without the efficiency that had followed the new trainer's efforts Mr. Spurgeon might have laughed to scorn McPhee's enthusiasm, but when such amazing results attended it, he was convinced. He had received practical proof of what loyalty could do. And there was this to be said, also – once he had got used to McPhee's extraordinary appearance, he had liked the fellow. He had learned, moreover, that McPhee could have gone to one of the best-paid jobs in football if only he had liked – after that Samuel Spurgeon had exploded.

Once outside in the cool air, however, he began to fear that he had been a fool, that he had allowed his new-found heart to run away with his head. This was the first act of Don Quixotry to his credit. It was trying work.

'Mac,' he said, 'you heard what I said?' The trainer nodded. 'I mean it – I'm going on with it! My daughter made me promise. But it's a hell of a job! It may ruin me! Let's find Howard. He'll be on our side, and he's the boy we want.'

Howard was not at his newspaper office – he was an evening paper man – but a smile and a nod from the old man guarding the right of way to the smelly regions above put the trailers on the right track. They found him, as prophesied, in the cosy bar-parlour of the "Blue Boar."

The sporting editor of *The Downside Evening Echo* stared when he say the pair enter. Instantly he was on his feet, his eyes questioning, everything else forgotten.

'Something's happened,' he said; I can see it for myself. The question is, are you going to tell me?'

'Of course we are!' boomed the mammoth Spurgeon, 'but let's have a drop of old brandy before I begin. When I tell you the story, "Happy," your blinkin' hat'll fall off…

'Drink your brandy!' replied the reporter, much as he would have spoken to a troublesome child. But he led the way to a deserted corner of the room.

'I was just coming along to the ground,' he started, when Samuel Spurgeon clutched him convulsively by the arm.

'Frank, you're a friend of Mac's here, aren't you?'

'Sure thing!' promptly replied *The Echo* man. 'Mac and me are blood-brothers! Why?'

'Then you're a friend of mine!' put in Spurgeon. 'I shall *want* you to be a friend, too, Frank; I've gone and done it!' he wheezed.

'Done what?' gasped Howard, startled out of his usual composure.

'Let me tell the story, Mr. Spurgeon, while ye finish your wee drappie,' put in McPhee. Then, without waiting for the permission he went on: 'Howard, Mr. Spurgeon has juist done a gran' thing for the Downside Club,' and he proceeded to tell the story of the evening's dramatic happenings.

'Hot stuff!' murmured the reporter. 'Won't Nancy be proud of you! I've nothing to do with the morning paper but I must get back to the office with this…

'Not yet!' choked the man who had defied circumstances, in combination with the rest of the Downside directors, that evening. 'I want your help, Frank, I tell you. I did this for old Mac here! He's a man, and I wasn't going to be such a dirty dog as to let the team that he has done so much for simply fade away. Do you know that he's got a standing offer to go to the Swifts as a coach – ?'

'*What!*' screamed Howard. 'The Swifts! Mac! You're made! When are you going?'

'I'm not going,' was the quiet reply.

'Of course he's not going!' spluttered Mr. Spurgeon. 'Haven't I just told you that I'm going to carry on? How could I do it without old Mac, here? He promised me he wouldn't go to the Swifts so long as there was a club in Downside.'

'Quite! Quite!' said the journalist quickly, almost irritably, as though he were already forming in his head the first sentences he was later to write. 'Man!' he suddenly exclaimed with electrifying vivacity. 'It's a great thing — a simply great thing!'

Seeing Mr. Spurgeon looking questioningly at him, he went on to explain his outburst.

'Downside couldn't do a thing for itself when it was living — not until you came along, anyway, Mac — but it can do a whole lot for itself now that it's supposed to be dead!' he cried excitedly. 'Now, don't get nervous, Mr. Spurgeon. If you'll just allow me another minute or so I'll tell you exactly what I mean. Start a shilling fund!' he cried triumphantly.

'A grand idea!'

Even the stoical McPhee allowed his voice to rise above the ordinary level as the words left he reporter's lips. From this point he felt convinced that he knew what was in Howard's mind. And he proved to be right.

'Don't you see?' cried Howard, almost hysterically, turning to Mr. Spurgeon, who was looking at him in bewilderment. 'Let me tell the true story about this, and everybody in the town who has an ounce of sportsmanship in them will help you! Especially when I tell 'em that McPhee, the man at whom — excuse me, old man — everybody used to laugh — all except a few of us, that is — has turned down that fine offer from the Swifts in order to stick by Downside.

'To-morrow I'll get the consent of the owners of *The Echo* to start a shilling fund for the Club. The very novelty of the scheme will make it a success — you see if it doesn't. We'll start all the pretty girls collecting. Every subscriber of ten shillings can have a share in the Club. Even if times are hard, men will go without their tobacco to help this *new* Downside — you see if I'm not right Now I must get back to write it — this is the greatest football story I've ever handled in Downside.'

Snatching up his hat, Howard bolted out of the room, leaving Mr. Spurgeon and McPhee staring at each other.

'Whisky this time,' wheezed Spurgeon, and to McPhee, 'Things look better, son!'

If it had been announced that the Prince of Wales and all his brothers had signed on as forwards for the Downside Football Club, the effect could not have been much more convulsive or far-reaching than was the case when the town read the next day of the dramatic re-birth of the local club. *The Echo's* article started the biggest sensation ever known in Downside football.

Howard proved himself an able psychologist. In short, what he had predicted came true. Letters poured in on the sporting editor of *The Evening Echo*, applauding him for "taking up the cudgels for true sportsmanship," as one writer expressed it, and saying such things about Mr. Spurgeon that that worthy was afraid to open the paper for the next few days.

There was no doubt the heart of Downside was touched. It had held in contempt the football club which took its name from the town, but now that the team had been rescued from the very jaws of death, it awaited a chance to offer its aid.

This chance came in *The Downside Evening Echo* Shilling Fund. The appeal which Howard made to the workers of the town and district through the columns of his paper was answered in the enthusiastic way which the reporter had predicted. The response, indeed, was astonishing; rather than allow the Club to die, the men of Downside must have gone without not only their tobacco, but their beer. Their imagination had been touched. Incidentally, *The Echo* became at once the most popular paper in Downside, so that Howard did not work for empty honour alone.

Proffers of help were not restricted to money. Men who had hitherto held aloof now came forward to consult with Samuel Spurgeon, and presently it was announced that, heavy as was the responsibility, a sufficient number of local sportsmen had consented to act, under the chairmanship of Mr. Spurgeon, as directors of the New Downside Football Club, as the Club was now universally called.

The standing of these men caused the high dignitaries of the bank — the same potentates who held the deeds of the Downside ground in their strong-room — to adopt a different tone. It seemed that, so far as they personally were concerned, the money market had become easier; in any case, they did not utter any more threats about being reluctantly forced to call their money in.

The days were full of surprises. Tranter, Hart, Daly and Simister had all gone to their new clubs — each making a point of coming to wish McPhee good-bye before he went — but Tommy Trott did not go.

He turned up at the dressing-room just after young Daly had left, and the trainer crossed to the door at once. The other partings had been hard, but this one would be the hardest of the lot. There had been a kinship between Trott and himself. Trott was the man who had saved him when otherwise he would have been lost. McPhee could not forget that fact.

'Weel, here's wishing you luck, Tommy!' he said, stretching out his hand. 'There's nae need to tell ye how sorry I am you're goin'.'

'But I'm *not* going!' He looked at McPhee quizzically.

'You're no goin'!' replied McPhee dully. 'But Middlesbridge have got your transfer, haven't they?'

'They thought they had. But I told their manager flat that I hadn't the slightest interest in Middlesbridge, that I had just bought a nice little tobacconist's business here in Downside, and that rather than go to his club I'd chuck football altogether. I had a benefit last year – a darned poor one, let me add – and I can rub along. No, I'm not going to Middlesbridge.'

'What –!' the trainer had started, when Trott slapped him on the back.

'Mac, old son,' he said. 'There was a time when the thing I wanted most was to leave this measly Club – well, now I want to stay with it. Funny, isn't it? Officially, my intention is to leave football, give up the game; unofficially, I'm still a Downside player – see?'

'Tommy,' replied McPhee, a flush in his weather-beaten face, 'this means a lot to me. And ye'll tak' on the captaincy again?'

'Mister Manager – I've heard all about your promotion – you can count me in on that, too – *and I'll try to play football now!*' Tommy Trott made a mock obeisance – perhaps to hide his real feelings – and left the dressing-room with a wave of the hand. He felt it wouldn't have been safe to stay longer.

Strenuous days followed. It was a case of working-the-clock-round for almost everyone concerned. Yet none worked so hard as the man who had been appointed to the dual position of trainer-manager of Downside. He had to make a new team out of practically nothing, for, with the exception of Tommy Trott, all his best players had been taken from him. The reserves the Club possessed were but the rawest of material.

Amid the flurry and worry of this nerve-racking reconstruction came the draw for the first round of the English Cup. The first two names out of the F.A. "Hat" were:

Downside v. Loam County

The bare printed words can convey no significance of what they really meant. For twenty years a fierce and relentless feud had existed between the two clubs. Fate had conspired to this end; Downside and Loam County had climbed into the First Division together, together they had dropped from that Kingdom of the Football Elite.

Near, but bitter neighbours, the meetings between the two clubs in the League had always been characterised by play that never slackened, play in which quarter was neither asked for, nor expected. These games thrilled the blood, and the general tension was such that even the rival directors could scarcely speak normally to each other. Years had but added to the hate, not softened the enmity.

And now, for the first time in history, the rivals had been drawn together in the Cup.

The Downside players had been resting after a strenuous afternoon's practice – the training had gone on all day since the reconstruction of the Club – when the news came through. It was Howard who sent it speeding over the telephone to McPhee.

'If you can only *beat* 'em,' the reporter had ejaculated.

McPhee had not replied. He was never a talker, particularly in tense moments. When he returned to the impatiently waiting footballers, he addressed them briefly, almost curtly, as a businesslike general might have done on the eve of an important battle.

'Lads,' he said, 'ye'll be playing Loam County – here. That will gi'e ye a wee bit o' advantage. I'll no ask the impossible, ye ken, but what I do expect is that ye'll train hard, and do everythin' I ask and that ye'll no groomble.'

A few hours later McPhee vouchsafed a few more words on the subject. A meeting of the directors had been called to discuss the prospects of this all-important game, and the manager-trainer had been asked for his opinion of the best team he could put in the field.

'I should be a fule if I said it was onything but puir,' he said. 'Take the old forward line; there is left only Trott at inside- right and Martin at inside-left. Ye'll understan' I ha'e to find substitutes for two good wingers, and a fairish centre-forward – and what I've got is not guid enough. With Simister gone, there is also a conseederable weakness at right-half. I'll do what I can, and the lads are willin' enough – but they have no the necessary skeel or experience the noo. It's my duty to tell ye the facts, gentlemen – the truth.'

'And it's the truth we want, McPhee. It isn't always pleasant, but it's invariably useful!' commented Mr. David Johnston, the new vice-chairman. 'Eh? What's that?' he turned to the youth who had been doing voluntary clerical work for the Club now that Ovens had been definitely relieved of his duties. This honorary secretary *pro. tem.*, had entered the board-room after knocking. He carried a card in his hand. This was taken by the chairman.

'The Rev. John Hunter,' read out Spurgeon. 'Who's he and what does he want?'

'I ha'e no' doot but what it'll be the Rev. John Hunter who used to play half-back for Wilmington Wanderers,' suggested McPhee instantly.

'But what can he want?' went on Samuel Spurgeon, whose heart was now thoroughly sound, but who – as he freely confessed himself – was not so mentally alert as he would like to be.

'Have him in and see, Mr. Chairman,' suggested Johnston.

'Show Mr. Hunter in,' wheezed Spurgeon, as he settled himself in his chair.

If the modern English Church Militant had desired to send a representative to a World Congress it could not have chosen a better type than the man who shortly afterwards entered the Downside F.C. board room. The Rev. John Hunter had mixed sport with his Christianity ever since his schoolboy days. A cleric who personified the value of a sound mind in a sound body, at thirty-seven years of age he was as fit a man as could have been found in the four countries.

Since his 'Varsity days Association Football had been his absorbing hobby. He had played for the Corinthians, for England, and for that famous team of Cup fighters, Wilmington Wanderers. When a bishop, anxious to achieve press notoriety, had delivered a scathing attack on professional football at a Church Congress, the Rev. John Hunter, a plain parson, had defended the paid player with such uncompromising vigour that his lordship had been routed with heavy loss. 'I have played with the professional football player, and I know him to be a good fellow – and a clean sportsman!' the Rev. John Hunter said, and the meeting had cheered him.

This, then, was the man who now stepped into the board room of the Downside Club, and looked round with shrewd but kindly eyes.

Once McPhee had set the memories of his directors searching, every man in the room now suddenly recalled that the Rev. John Hunter had won an English International shirt ten years before.

'Sit down, Mr. Hunter,' said the vice-chairman, 'I need not say how very pleased we are to make your acquaintance. We in Downside are always ready to give a welcome to such a sportsman as yourself.'

'That's very kind of you. But I'm sure, gentlemen, that you must all be asking yourselves, 'What does this fellow want?' Well, I'll tell you – and that will be my excuse for thrusting myself on you in this fashion to-night.'

Tossing his hat to another chair, the visitor continued: 'I'm shortly coming to Downside to work. The living of St. Martin's has been offered to me, and because I think I may be of some use here, I have accepted it. Now, I've followed the recent career of your Club with a great deal of interest. If you will allow me to say so, gentlemen, I think the action you have taken in saving the old club was one of splendid sportsmanship. You are short of experienced players, I understand, and you are on the eve of an intensely exciting Cup Tie, the winning of which I can quite understand would mean a great deal to you. I'm little better than an old crock now, I'm afraid – but, well, if I can be of any use to you, I shall be pleased to turn out against Loam County. Strictly on merit, you understand – your trainer must decide that.'

'Mon, that's fine of you!'

McPhee, as before, had been the first to realise the possibilities. He spoke as a man deeply moved.

Then a clamour arose. Only a fortnight before, the Rev. John Hunter had turned out for the Corinthians against a well-known London League club, and the critics had reported him as having played a wonderful game considering his age. Here was a sportsman indeed!

The Rev. John Hunter politely deprecated all the fuss that was being made – and then sprang another surprise.

'My real offer is to come, gentlemen,' he said. 'You may or may not know that the people of young Aplin, who played such a fine game for Oxford against Cambridge this year, live just outside Downside – at Merrywood. I have played with Aplin myself twice recently – he has turned out for the Corinthians, you know – and he is very good indeed. Now, the point is, I think I could persuade him to turn out with me if – if you could do with him.'

'Where does he play?' This from Spurgeon.

'Outside-right,' promptly replied that football encyclopaedia, Angus McPhee. 'Could we *do* wi' him, Mr. Hunter? Why, mon, he'd be worth his weight in gold to us juist noo! And ye say he's really guid?' The trainer looked at the old International keenly.

'I think I know a wing-player when I see one,' said Hunter, 'at least I ought to do. With two exceptions Aplin is the best outside-right I have seen play this season.'

'Mon! – get him!' cried Angus McPhee. 'Send him along to me, and I'll get to work on him!'

Two mornings later Charles Aplin, pronouncedly amateur, came to the Downside ground escorted by his friend and mentor, the Rev. John Hunter. He was rather shy, somewhat embarrassed, mildly amused, at his first glimpse of Angus McPhee, but very willing. Like his parson pal, he was a sportsman, and although he could have played for practically any team in the country, from Aston Villa downwards, after he had listened to the story Hunter told him, he was eager to do his bit for Downside — especially as John Hunter would be the half-back working behind him.

The Downside pros. viewed the widely-cut football knickers and the handkerchief[5] carried in the left hand of this gilded amateur with mingled amusement and dismay, until Aplin showed them that in the art of controlling a football he could leave most of them standing.

Gaunt, almost forbidding, McPhee commanded the 'Varsity stripling to essay flying runs down the touch-line with the ball, to centre whilst travelling at top speed, to take corner-kicks, and to shoot from the wing.

At the end he drew the Rev. John Hunter unceremoniously towards him, and said in a tone of fierce content: 'Mon, he's all ye said!'

Hunter, who loved an enthusiast, beamed in response.

On the Wednesday night before the Cup-Tie, the following team was announced as that selected to carry the Downside colours against Loam County:

| Camp. |
Giles. Gerrish.
J. Hunter. Dixon. Harrigan.
C. R. Aplin. Trott. Gilligan. Martin. Finlay.

There were several weak spots, but it was the best that could be done.

Then on the following day – Thursday – came one of those shocks which threaten to shorten the life of the true football enthusiast.

Walter Camp, the Downside goalkeeper, was stated to have been ordered to bed by the Club doctor, suffering from influenza.

Eagerly Downside read on. Who would take Camp's place? When they saw the name it seemed to have become italicised.

It was *McPhee*.

---

[5] There are accounts of amateur international Walter Corbett (1908 Olympic gold medallist) always carrying a handkerchief when he was on the field.

CHAPTER XIV

McPHEE SAVES A PENALTY

As in France, so in Downside; the name McPhee became a legend. It carried a meaning; it had a significance. Those who did not know McPhee before, knew him now. With his finger on the pulse of public opinion, Frank Howard re-told the story of Angus McPhee's coming to Downside, and of the many startling changes that had succeeded his arrival.

The feeling was one of confidence. It seems preposterous, yet it was so. Had any other football official in England been placed between the Downside goalposts, the outcry would have kept honest folk from sleeping; but it seemed to be fit and proper that the man who had done so much to save the Club should guard its goal on this, perhaps the most momentous day in its history. Especially after *The Evening Echo* reporter pledged his word that, in spite of the limp which McPhee carried as a legacy from the War, the trainer-manager was indubitably the best man, in the absence of Walter Camp, to keep goal for Downside against Loam County.

'But for his War injury, and his undoubted genius as a coach, McPhee would have made a great name for himself as a player,' asserted Howard. 'That is the unanimous opinion of the whole of the present Downside team.'

It had, indeed, been no sudden fit of vanity that had caused McPhee to pick himself for the responsible post of goalkeeper. The plain truth was that Camp's sudden illness had created very real consternation in the Downside Board Room. Downing, the reserve goalkeeper, was an untried youngster, whose nerves would be sure to go back on him. They had already done so in a reserve match (a hole-in-the-corner "friendly" with a local Suburban League eleven), so that it would be frankly suicidal to pick him.

Spurgeon, at his wits' end, had turned in open despair to the manager. 'What do you say to *this?*' he asked in a cold-is-the-gloomy-tomb voice.

'Wi' the directors' permeesion, I'm going to play mysel',' was the reply.

'*You* – but you're not a registered player – you're not a player at all, Mac. Holy Joe! This is no time for joking!' Spurgeon's whale-like frame shook like a monster blanc-mange.

'I'm serious.' McPhee's cold, matter-of-fact tone testified to it. 'The first thing I did when you appointed me manager was to register my name as a Downside player. I did it as a puirly precautionary measure, ye'll understan', on the preenciple that ye never know what ye may want.

'The only poseetion I could hope to fill was goal, and I shall no' fill that unless I satisfy the lads that I am a better mon than young Downing. Come doon to the ground and see for yersel'.'

Spurgeon went down. Once again McPhee, like the mariner in the poem, was holding him with his glittering eye. The two went into the dressing-room together.

'Lads,' stated McPhee, looking round to see if Downing, the reserve goalkeeper, was present, and feeling thankful that he was not, as he wished to spare the lad's feelings. 'Camp's gone sick, and I daren't trust Downing. He's over young and he's no experienced enough for a match like this.' There was a pause. The players looked at each other in consternation.

'The trouble is, there's no one else – except mysel'. Ye'll all be laughin' at the thought of me in goal? But come on oot – you and Mr. Spurgeon shall decide. I'll no' peek mysel'.'

When fully garbed in his football clothes he certainly looked as though he might be a goalkeeper. In his jersey and shorts he was awe-inspiring – once you conquered the tendency to laugh.

'Now, lads,' he said, when he stood alone in the goal, 'ye'll just shoot and never mind my infirmity.'

One of the practice balls came to the crafty foot of Tommy Trott. The forward flicked it almost tenderly, and gently pushed it forward. Then, putting his whole body into the shot (a sure sign of a real player) he aimed at the far corner. It was a beautifully-driven ball. At that range – fifteen yards – it looked unstoppable, but with a sudden, if ungainly, dive, McPhee, the emergency man of Downside, got to the ball, and sent it spinning round the post.

Even Trott stared. He knew that McPhee wanted a real testing; that the manager would give the rough edge of his tongue to anyone who endeavoured to let him down lightly. That was why he had put everything he knew into that opening shot.

And McPhee had saved it!

After that there came shots high and low, fast and slow, straight and curling; from the wing, and from the penalty spot. To say that the goalkeeper on trial saved them all would be merely to excite the scornful laughter of the sophisticated; but several times McPhee caused the marksmen to stare in amazement.

True, he had remarkable reach and unusual height, yet these alone did not explain it. The new goalkeeper had a mind inside his body and an almost uncanny sense of anticipation. The reason why a footballer makes a success is generally because he *thinks* about his work. McPhee had long since accepted football as a science. Now that he stood in goal on trial, he applied to his own play the same principles which, in the case of Camp, had yielded such good results. Had not good goal- keepers been plentiful in the land, it is almost a certainty that some team would have made a bid for the services of Camp at the recent "auction-sale."

Twenty minutes' fierce fusillade told everyone – McPhee included – who was to keep goal against Loam County.

Bedlam started on the morning of the match. The supporters of Loam County arrived by early trains thousands strong. Profusely decorated with blue and white favours, they paraded the streets, flaunting their blatant confidence like a red cloak before a bull.

These passionate pilgrims brought with them their own atmosphere. The air of Downside had been surcharged before, but now it was electric. Downside knew its team might be better, but it resented being told so... There was one exceedingly painful affair in the High Street; but after that, the police had the situation fairly well in hand.

By one o'clock the streets were comparatively clear of the ribald men of Loam. Those who weren't in the eating-houses were on their way to the Downside ground – catch them being late on a day like this, when the gates might be shut half an hour before the kick-off...

The tenseness increased with every minute. At a quarter to two o'clock, twenty-five thousand people were already inside the Downside enclosure. The greater proportion of these would seem to have overlooked their regular dinner, for the huge ring round the playing pitch was white with paper bags into which fingers eagerly dipped.

These fingers went instinctively to the bags, for there were no eyes to guide them – all eyes were fixed on the marked-out splash of greenish-brown turf, with great bare patches in it here and there, on which the forthcoming duel of feet and brains would shortly be fought.

Through the frantically-clicking turnstiles further crowds poured. Although there was plenty of room left in all parts except the two stands (where all the seats had been sold days before) they could not content themselves by walking. Urged by an uncontrollable and yet undefinable force, they could only express their present feelings by – *running!* Some looked unseeingly at watches which they carried open in their hands, and then asked each other the time. There were still forty minutes before the kick-off...

Already, however, the aristocrats of the game are sinking into their envied grand-stand seats. Roars of laughter now. Helped over the railings by eager hands, the official mascot of Loam County made a mock obeisance to the crowd, and then solemnly strutted over to the centre of the playing pitch. He was an aged, badly-crippled miner – Loam being a mining town – grotesquely garbed in royal blue football jersey, white knickers (over ordinary trousers), and football boots so plastered with white laces that the leather was nearly invisible.

He was later joined by his assistants – two lesser workers in the realms of mascotry, who had contented themselves by merely donning fancy costumes of blue and white stripes. The three solemnly tested both goal-nets amid the delighted cheering of the Loam contingent, and the affected scorn of the Downside supporters.

'Where's the goat? Let's have the goat!' yelled the home crowd.

The cry penetrated even into the dressing-room. The minds of the directors, who were already present giving an anxious and critical eye to each man's condition, were too preoccupied to listen to this idle clamour, but McPhee, although the most heavily-worked man in the room, and the one whose shoulders carried the greatest responsibility, turned to his assistant.

'Ye'll see George about Neb,' he said. 'Let him take the goat round. The more the crowd laughs the better temper they'll be in.'

So the mascotry odds were levelled. One goat against three men seemed a grotesque disproportion, but Neb was much the funnier to look at... The crowd threatened to go mad when they saw him.

Every minute was ticked off now. The impatient crowd fretted and fumed, and muttered: 'I wonder when they'll be out?' In the Downside dressing-room the waiting seemed intolerable. Having seen to all his charges personally, although the assistant trainer, a man of considerable experience, was there, McPhee proceeded to get into his own things. Once ready, his mind passed back naturally to those fretting moments before he went over the top for the first time in France. And yet he was sure he did not feel quite as wound-up then as now...

'Try to remember what I've told ye, lads. Dinna be afraid – they're no' much to beat – and keep hold of yoursel's!'

That was all. Then he lapsed into his own thoughts again. He had much to think about. The directors had brought him news that the crowd promised to be a record one; already they were packed like sardines in the enclosures, while the flower-pot stands were swaying like saplings in a gale…

A record crowd! Here certainly was encouragement. No doubt many had come because a Cup-Tie, no matter how bad the two teams competing, has a compelling power peculiar to itself. There were thousands of rabid Loam partisans present. Others had probably come merely out of curiosity. No matter! They had come! Their interest had been stirred; and if Downside could only win that day, their interest could be preserved and sustained.

But his football sense told McPhee that in any case Downside would be lucky even to draw that afternoon, while to win – yes, but strange things had happened in Cup-Ties before. Had not Hull City beaten Middlesborough 5-0 and Crystal Palace whipped Everton by six clear goals?'

"The sooner we do it, the sooner we're dead!" hummed someone at the door. The warbler was Mr. Richard Hartley, the merriest wag, but the best referee on the F.A. list.

'Be good boys, and I shan't smack any of you!' he said, as the scarlet-jerseyed players filed past him, with Tommy Trott in front and the gaunt, lean form of Angus McPhee bringing up the rear.

A strident roar greeted the County players from the throats of the Loam supporters, seeming to fill the home dressing-room with sound. But the welcome to the visitors was but a zephyr compared with the shout that the home crowd lifted out of their systems when Downside showed themselves.

It was a white-faced group of players for the most part when they first showed themselves; but that roar of welcome brought the colour into the faces of some of the younger Downside players. Still, these football knightlings twitched as they lined up for the kick off.

Tommy Trott had lost the toss – a fact which served for a tearing upheaval of noise from the Loam section of the crowd. There was not much in it, however – no sun and only a slight wind blowing down the field in the direction of the country end goal which Downside defended.

The Loam players grinned at each other as they stopped the preliminary "kick-in," and faced their opponents. If Downside stood for diffidence, Loamshire were all confidence.

Jauntily, almost leisurely, they started. We might as well get a goal straight away, they seemed to say – and they nearly did. Centre-half to centre-forward; centre-forward to outside-right; outside-right (after beating Harrigan, the Downside left-half) to inside-right; inside-right (after fooling Gerrish, the Downside left-back) to centre-forward again, and then – *bang!*

'Goal! 'hysterically called the passionate pilgrims from Loam, and, by the old boots of Bobby Templeton, they had every reason but one to call the magic word.

Every reason but one! It was a splendid shot, splendidly directed. But in that urgent second which counted, a long, gaunt, uncomely form in the Downside goal hurled himself sideways – and the ball sped off the tips of his ungloved fingers round the post for a corner. As McPhee had saved from Trott, the Downside crack, in practice, so had he saved now from Haytor, the Loam County crack.

Thudding cheers, mingled with exclamations of profane wonder from the Loam supporters, and then the dangerously-curling ball from the corner kick. Again the emergency man of Downside predominated.

Rising high above every other fierce-struggling contestant, his gaunt form could be seen, sombre in its black jersey. A fist was thrust out, a mighty lunge and that curling ball, so laden with danger, was punched clear. It fell at the feet of John Hunter, at right-half, who, after dribbling three yards, sent it swirling down the field.

The home goal had been saved. Eyes went to the lank form in all black, standing in the Downside gateway. To many, McPhee had been nothing more than a name before, almost a myth; now he was a reality, a living force.

Some men have a personality that radiates confidence. McPhee in his goalkeeper's garb, looked efficient, if grotesque. One man casting shrewd looks at him gave it as his firm opinion that 'that feller ain't such a fool as he looks.' That seemed to express it.

The goalkeeper could be relied upon. But the rest of the team? The backs were sound, the halves worked like beavers with John Hunter always the outstanding figure for all his thirty-seven years, but the forwards were undeniably weak.

Aplin, on the right wing, had so far been a complete failure. He was palpably nervous, and obviously very anxious to do well. But the importance of the occasion was plainly too much for him. This was his first experience of professional football, and the frenzy of the crowd worried him, and put him off his game. So much was plain to McPhee, watching from the Downside goalmouth. Yet the fact did not, as it might have been thought, considering how he knew he must rely on that right wing, unduly depress him. The game was young yet.

None of the other forwards, except Trott, who was too much of a veteran to have nerves, even when the match was a Cup-Tie against Loam County, had settled down. They were passing wildly, over-running the ball and centring behind, instead of in front, of goal. Indeed, they were forgetting practically everything that their coach had so persistently dinned into their ears for a fortnight past. One fact, however, stood out prominently even among their most glaring faults; the whole team was perfectly trained, and every man was desperately keen.

After ten minutes or so, the play underwent a change. Had the Downside goal fallen in that dazzling opening burst of the Loam forwards, the game might have developed into a rout; the spirit of these untried recruits might have been broken. But the indomitable spirit of the man in goal seemed to reach out to them. More and more confidence characterised the work of the home men as time went on, and with this confidence came fewer mistakes.

Particularly was this noticeable on the Downside right. From the start John Hunter, his face grim-set, but his eyes alight with the excitement of the sport, had played solid, steady football, not doing anything very brilliant, but making no mistakes, and giving the Loam left winger, the "star" forward of the County, not an inch of rope. Already he was a warm favourite with the crowd.

Certainly this player was justifying the faith and trust which McPhee had put in him. Not only did he most efficiently "police" the County's most dangerous raider, but he looked after his protégé, Aplin, like a father. Once, when the young 'Varsity winger had drooped his head in bitter disappointment after he had mistimed a pass horn the half-back, Hunter patted him on the back to restore his confidence. The crowd cheered the incident.

Another man might have lost patience with Aplin. Time after time he broke down. But Hunter knew the real worth of the amateur winger, and he persisted in feeding him.

At last both the half-back and the crowd got their reward. John Hunter swept another inviting ball forward. It fell plump at the feet of Aplin.

'Hold it!' shouted the half-back, and Aplin held it.

As though confidence had suddenly come to him, he sprang at once into a dribble. The left-half came plunging towards him, anxious to knock this gilded amateur, with the handkerchief in the left hand, into the enclosure; but Aplin was "away" this time, swerving most wonderfully without losing control of the ball.

'Good boy, Appy!' shrieked the crowd. The boy had found his form, and the crowd a pet-name at one and the same time.

With his pronounced amateur style, Aplin was a "picture player." He ran with grace, and played with ease. His speed was astonishing; tipping the ball past the County back, he outraced the defender, steadied the ball on the very line, and volleyed over a very dream of a centre.

The ball came breast-high to Trott. The Downside captain promptly dropped to one knee, twisted his dark head – and the ball pinged away. Only a marvellous leap by the County goalkeeper prevented it from entering the net at the far corner.

'Come along, you bonny boys!'

The crowd had held its breath while that palpitating siege lasted, but now it eased its lungs. The cheers had a tonic effect upon the raw youths of Downside. Again Downside went raiding. From Hunter to Trott, and from Trott to Aplin, the ball sped. Craft had been restored to the amateur's toes now; that first successful run of his had chased away his former broodings and disappointment. He cut away again while the crowd roared his name.

This time, however, he did not hug the touch-line. Instead, when the half-back had been foiled, he dribbled inwards. Only when the whole of the County defence had converged on him, did he loose the ball. Then his right foot moved quickly – and the ball was back-heeled neatly to the waiting Trott who had taken up position.

'Shoot, Tommy!' shrieked the crowd.

It was a dazzle-drive, a raking shot. A few inches lower, and no goalkeeper on earth could have retrieved that ball, but in its flight it must have gathered loft, for instead of entering the net, it struck the cross-bar with such force that it re-bounded to beyond the penalty area.

Heartening work! One of the visitors was temporarily knocked out through heading a powerful return by one of the Downside backs, and McPhee left his goal to confer with his team.

Within five minutes of the referee throwing up the ball, Downside had taken the lead!

This was the way of it. A free kick was awarded the home team. Hunter took it. Looking round, he waved up Harrigan, the left-half, as though he meant to pass the ball to him. Then he kicked – but it was his left foot, instead of his right, which he used – and the ball instead of being "hit" hard, was gently tapped out to the right.

It came bouncing gently to the right foot of Aplin. Without wasting a moment, the amateur shot fiercely in a first-time drive.

It was one of those shots which the Corinthians copyrighted years ago. Miller, in the County goal, had obviously not expected Aplin to shoot – but then, the whole scheme had been consummated within such a short space of time that the goal-keeper might quite justifiably have pleaded complete ignorance. It is certain he knew nothing about this shot that scored almost from the touch-line. It was not until the ball was actually in the net that full realisation came.

Indeed, it was not until then that the crowd grasped what had happened. When it did, amazing scenes occurred. The vast majority had come, if not to scoff, certainly to be amused. They had been during the first quarter of an hour – but this, this was *football!*

The transports of delight were not confined to the crowd; on the field the Downside players were shaking hands with each other with such boisterous zest that each man might have just come into a fortune. Had the man who scored been a brother professional, they would have smothered him with their congratulations; as it was, they bestowed these on each other. But Aplin was not allowed to escape the general rejoicing. John Hunter clapped him jubilantly on the back, and McPhee's long legs scuttled down the playing pitch, and the crowd cheered again as the manager shook the scorer by the hand.

After this, more frenzy. What they had, Downside meant to hold. They were playing confidently now – that perfectly-shot goal had been a wonderful stimulus to them.

Their opponents had changed their own mood. From early confidence, they had now passed to desperation. Astonishing insolence for Downside to have scored the first goal! Preposterous position that they – Loam County – should be behind! The visiting centre-half, the captain of the team, clapped his hands in exhortation, and the men of Loam rallied, exerting all their craft, all their skill, and all their vigour.

It was a furious fight. Territorially, Loam had the advantage, but the Downside defence would not yield. Giles and Gerrish were still crude, but under the tutelage of McPhee, they had mastered their former faults. Besides, they had their coach immediately behind, shouting instructions in his Glasgow brogue. The knowledge that McPhee was there made them attempt the impossible – and often they brought it off!

So time passed, with the thrills coming at the rate of three a minute. Many times the hearts of the Downside supporters leapt into their mouths, but not once with such sudden quickness as when, five minutes from resting-time, Haytor, the Loam centre- forward, came tearing a passage through both home backs.

There was only McPhee now. The latter stood for one second, sizing up the situation, and then, his limp very apparent, rushed forward himself, and fell straight at the feet of the on-rushing raider.

His sure hands gripped the ball which he had whipped off the very toes of the centre-forward. The crowd saw that – but little more, for the next second McPhee was the centre of a frantic scrimmage. The crowd did not know that he held on to the ball until his hands were a mass of bruises, that when he finally Bung the ball clear, by ill-chance it cannoned off the body of Giles, the Downside right back, and from thence on to the foot of a Loam forward who promptly banged it into the empty net They did not know these facts; all that was clear to them was the score, 1-1. Scarcely had the ball been centred before the half-time whistle went.

'*Mac!* – your hands, man' Trott gasped as he saw what the Loam forwards, in their anxiety to get the ball in that recent desperate scrimmage in the Downside goal-mouth, had done to the Scot's hands. They were raw and bleeding where they weren't bruised.

McPhee waved him aside. 'Ye were leempin', Tommy, in the last ten minutes, What's the trouble? It's ye who's got to get the goals next half, remember! Now, lads, listen to me a minute.'

While the Downside men sucked their lemons, McPhee talked. He reviewed the forty-five minutes of football that had just passed as a military student might have reviewed a battle. He told his listeners of the weaknesses of the opposition, and how they – Downside – must try to exploit those weaknesses for their own advantage.

'We're the better trained team, lads,' he said, 'and we shall last the longer. Now start off the second half wi' a rush. Try to run them clean off their legs, and play to the left wing practically all that time – Mr. Aplin, ye will please remember that ye are bein' starved on pairpose, seestematically, during this period. Tommy,' turning to Trott, 'it's guid news to know that your leemp in the last ten minutes doesna seegnify verra much. But ye'll exaggerate that leemp when we go back; ye'll make the opposition believe that ye're crocked, you understan'. After a few minutes – and after makin' a rotten attempt to get to several passes (these, Mr. Hunter, will come from ye) ye'll change places with Mr. Aplin, and go on the wing. The Downside right wing will be practically 'feenished'; that is the impression I want Loam County to get, onyway.

'After twenty minutes or so, a centre must come across from the left wing. Ye will pretend to take it, Mr. Aplin, but ye will fumble the ball pairposely (all part o' a plan, ye onderstan'), and the ball will go to Trott. Then, Tommy – it will be up to ye – but we must get the next goal!'

'Right!' cut in the Downside inside-right briskly, 'but, Mac, what about your hands?'

'What's wrong wi' my hands? Get on out there! That's the referee's whistle.'

According to plan! Eighteen minutes from the re-start Finlay, after eluding Wilton, the Loam County right back, swung over a square centre. Gilligan, the centre-forward, made to trap the ball, but instead merely allowed it to pass through his legs to the expectant Aplin, who had gone inside after Tommy Trott, to the utter dismay of the crowd, had limped to the wing, an obvious cripple.

The 'Varsity amateur dribbled a couple of yards, drew the defence and then, upon being tackled again, gently tapped the ball to the Downside captain, who had crept in from the wing, where nobody had troubled to mark him because he was apparently crocked. Trott seemed to have suddenly mislaid his limp.

Directly the ball came to his foot, he sprang to life. The left-back was so astounded that he made but a half-hearted attempt to check this unexpected raider, and Trott, dashing on, flashed the ball past the County goalkeeper before anyone but McPhee and the rest of the Downside team could realise what had happened.

2 – 1!

That schemed-for goal was like a bomb in the Loam camp. It shook them from goalkeeper to centre-forward. They looked like men who had been deceived in life as they lined up for the kick-off. They had a sour taste in their mouths. To be still a goal behind after declaring so much –!

They were terribly weary men by this time. The ache was in their limbs. They had been literally run to a standstill during the past twenty minutes; now they could only toil wearily after the ball.

Only one section remained steady. That was the defence. The Loam backs were the mainstay of the team, and now – to their credit – they valiantly shouldered their burden. Kicking like mules from any angle, and tackling with a fierce relentlessness, they staved off further disaster.

But they had the world on their shoulders, for, from now on, the game resolved itself into a continual attack on the Loam goal. Only rarely did the County cross the half-way line. Fretting and fuming Haytor, the visiting centre-forward, could be seen waiting for the chance to equalise.

It was not until the end of the game that he had his opportunity. Then the Downside centre-half failed to time a dropping ball and Haytor was away. A striking figure in action was the Loam centre-forward: squat, but powerfully built, he was one of the hardest men to knock off the ball in modern football. A "barger" who stopped at nothing – not even at the possibility of breaking his neck, he could always be regarded as dangerous when in full stride. Now he was rushing towards the Downside goal as though he were on fire.

Gerrish, the home left back, challenged him, but a vigorous shoulder-charge sent him purling – and Haytor stormed on. Giles made for him, missed, and then came tearing back. Just inside the penalty area, he flung himself again at the centre- forward. The latter went down in a heap.

Their hearts in their mouths once more, the crowd saw the Loam players dramatically appealing, and then the referee pointed to a certain dread mark.

'Penalty!'

The fatal word was whispered by some, shouted in frenzy by others.

A penalty it was. There was the Loam centre-half kicking the mud off his boots before placing the ball to his liking on the broad splash of whitewash – and, claiming all eyes again, was the tall, ungainly figure in all black poised as though for flight in the Downside goal.

All that had gone before paled before this tremendous moment. If Loam County equalised through that penalty kick, anything might still happen.

A silence as of death hung over the ground. Many were afraid to look. These were the supporters of Downside. Others craned their necks until they risked dislocating them. These were the men from Loam.

At length the Loam penalty-taker was ready. He stood up and grinned. Then he placed the ball more fastidiously to his liking on the mark. After that a short run back, a puzzling movement, and –

Deafening cheers! Hysterical cries, that could only have come from men thoroughly crazy and distraught.

A miracle had saved Downside, a miracle wearing a black jersey and black football knickers. In the moment that the Loam penalty-taker had rushed forward, McPhee, who had been studying the man, threw himself full length to the right, and in the same second he felt the ball strike his outstretched hands and twist itself over the line outside the goal post.

Whereupon the Downside players held a sort of reception in their goal-mouth. Because his hands were so sore and maltreated, the rest of the team had to be content with slapping the man who had saved his side on the back.

That was the end – the end of the thrills, if not of the play. That uncanny anticipation of the opposing goalkeeper broke the hearts of the County. Before they had been so leg-weary that they could scarcely raise another gallop. They had hoped to equalise through that kick from the spot, and then hold out to the end. Half a loaf was better than no bread, and the replay at Loam on the following Wednesday they would lay the dust with the Downside mob.

So they had reasoned, building castles which were toppled to the ground directly Angus McPhee turned aside that ball which had been aimed so deftly true for the right corner of the net, and which only a weird exhibition of anticipation had prevented from scoring.

2 –1!

That was a memorable night in Downside. Those who had not known Angus McPhee before, knew him now!

CHAPTER XV

THE £2000 LEFT FOOT

The Downside team were frolicking round McPhee in the dressing-room after the match like puppies round a fully-grown dog. Both by brain and hand he had won the Cup Tie for them, and they were endeavouring to show him their gratitude.

The room, large as it was, overflowed with people. They all seemed hilariously happy. The Rev. John Hunter, stripping off his scarlet jersey, covered with the mud of the playing pitch, crossed to the manager of Downside.

'I'm going to keep this – at least, until the next Cup-Tie, McPhee,' he said. 'It's a pleasure to play for a team like Downside. I've never seen a professional crowd quite like this,' and he motioned towards the victors, who were making no attempt to strip and get into the waiting warm baths, but still stood chatting in excited groups.

'Yes, it's been a gran' day – a richt gran' day, Mister Hunter,' acknowledged the Scot. 'Skeel will do much in football – but enthusiasm will do more – and these lads o' mine... why, I've worked 'em so hard that I'd no' be surprised if they hated the vairy sight of me, but they don't, I'm glad to know.'

'I should think not, man. I'm a blunt chap, not given overmuch to scratching any man's back, but you've *made* Downside – this team, and the one that was sold. My experience is that any professional looks up to a man who can beat him at his own job. That save of yours – well, no wonder they mobbed you! It was a remarkable bit of goalkeeping, McPhee.'

'I wouldna' say it was a' that, Mr. Hunter. It was simple enough, in a way. Ye see, I studied the mon's face, ye ken, and I knew from his eyes where he intended to aim – and I juist got there in time.'

'With those hands! Well, if I can be of any further help to you – and I speak for Aplin, too – you have only to let me know. Aplin was awfully bucked about getting that first goal.'

'If we get through to the Final, Mr. Hunter, ye'll be playin' at right-half,' was McPhee's reply, as he turned away to his duties.

The Final!
Preposterous as it seemed, McPhee's thoughts kept turning to that tantalising mirage. Deep down within him, he felt that, raw as it was, his team was destined to go far. Anything could happen in the Cup; the words had passed into a football proverb.

Downside would not go far because of its skill and craftsmanship – it lacked a great deal in these respects, and it would take him all his time to make good these deficiencies – but as he had told John Hunter, enthusiasm was almost as good an asset as skill. After this surprising win, there would not be a team in England so enthusiastic as Downside, the club that had been saved from itself. It was the very rawness of the side that created this enthusiasm. As for the older members of the team, like Trott and Harrigan, he felt he could rely on their loyalty to himself to do their bit

The play that afternoon might have been a great deal worse. Giles and Gerrish at back had made mistakes, but they would both improve. Hunter had strengthened the half-back line, and would continue to strengthen it now that he had promised to play for the rest of the season.

No – it had not been so bad; but he wanted an inside-left. Yes, he wanted an inside-left, and he wanted him badly.

'Shake hands with my old pal, Peter Dark, Mac!'

A touch on the arm aroused him from his reverie. Standing by the side of the Downside inside-right was an unmistakable old pro. This man had shot many goals before great crowds, unless he were mistaken.

'Don't grip too hard, Peter, old scout,' went on Trott. 'Mac's hands are all messed up – but he's worth a handshake all right.'

'That penalty save was,' commented the stranger crisply. 'Glad to meet you,' he added.

'Darkie, here,' explained the Downside inside-right, putting his hand on the other's shoulder, 'was with me in the Stars' team six years ago. Got a bushel of goals with that left foot of his! The Stars paid £2000 for it. Broke the record for transfer fees up till then, that £2000 did. Some inside-left, Darkie was – Lord! Mac, if we only had him in this team!'

McPhee did not immediately reply. This was only another of the occasions when he was saving his breath. He was first of all trying to estimate Peter Dark's age. Finally he put the man down at thirty-eight or thirty-nine – old for a footballer, especially for an inside forward. He would be bound to be slow – terribly slow – But, *Dark!* The man bore an illustrious name!

'Ha'e ye stopped playin' the noo?' he asked, with a casual air, which he found hard to affect.

'Had to!' said the other with grim terseness. 'Knee went – can't run, only hobble now. Nobody will look at me, and I can't afford to go to a big specialist. It would cost me a hundred quid, at least.'

'Pity! And you're nae sair old as that?'

'Thirty-eight next birthday! But it's only my knee – what about Billy Meredith, Rutherford, Dicky Bond – they're all as old, or older, than me. I looked after myself – Hell! I'd like just one more season. Damn this knee!'

The man spoke with concentrated bitterness. His words sounded out of place in that room so filled with the laughter of happy youth.

McPhee felt himself go out to this man. In him he could see one of the affecting tragedies of professional sport, a famous player broken on the wheel. Years ago he had been one of the great masters of the game, a man with such a famous left foot that a record transfer fee had been paid for its exclusive services. Then he had been an idol of the great crowds; now – no one wanted him; few remembered him.

McPhee saw Dark's eyes drinking in all the familiar scenes of a footballer's dressing-room, and watched the man's face stiffen as though he had suffered a spasm of pain. Sympathy welled up inside the Scot. Had he not been in a worse state than Peter Dark before Chance had drawn him to Downside? Perhaps –

'Going back hame to-night?' he asked the owner of the once-famous left foot. He did not know where Dark lived, of course.

'Going to put up with Tommy, and talk over old times, if he will have me.'

'Have you! Just sit down there and make yourself comfortable!' Trott's tone was that of an affectionate brother. He was evidently genuinely pleased to see his old comrade.

'Tommy, call in at my place some time to-morrow – and bring your frien',' said McPhee, and once more he turned to his work.

Peter Dark stripped in Angus McPhee's bedroom the following afternoon. He might have been about to undergo an examination for life insurance, only this thing was far more important to him than any amount of money being paid over to someone else at his death. Football was life to him, not death. The gaunt-faced Scot standing over him was going to see if he could bring him back to football. He hadn't said so in as many words, but his manner implied it.

The long, sensitive fingers which pried and probed about the wrecked knee would not have disgraced a surgeon. Their touch was soothing and yet searching. After twenty minutes, McPhee straightened his back.

'Mon, if ye'll step doon to the office the morrow's morn, I'll ha'e a professional form waiting for ye to sign,' he said.

'What? Are you going to get my knee right? Can I play football again?' The old International jumped up, and clutched the Downside manager's arm excitedly. There was an almost pathetic eagerness about him.

'Aye, if ye'll do what I shall want ye to do. In a month I hope to have ye right, Dark; wi' luck before.'

Rarely had a specialist's opinion given greater joy. Tommy Trott executed a *fandango* in the restricted space of the bedroom with such zest that the crockery became crazy and joined in the dance. Then came a shrill feminine whine from below.

'Mr. *McPhee!*'

For the first time in the experience of Tommy Trott, the manager of Downside exhibited signs of fear.

'Yon's my landlady,' he said; 'we'd better get doon – I shouldna like to offend her.'

Dutifully two of the cleverest inside forwards who ever touched a ball followed him.

McPhee lived up to his word in regard to Peter Dark, as he had done in so many other matters. In fact, he did more than merely keep his word. By the time the next Cup Tie arrived, "Happy" Howard announced to his delighted and expectant readers that the famous inside-left, Peter Dark, the man for whose wizard left foot the record sum of £2,000 had been paid by the Stars, some years before, had come back to football thoroughly sound, and that he would play for Downside Club regularly.

'Give 'em a "star" to play with!' is the saying of one of the greatest football managers that ever lived. What he meant was that you can keep a football crowd happy by including a player in your team whose name is something to conjure with, and whose play has passed into a legend. The football enthusiast has no use for a "star" that is definitely finished, but a "star" re-born…!

The night they read the news about Peter Dark, Downside could talk of nothing else.

Well might they talk of Peter Dark. Several months' absence from Big Football had thrust him out of the limelight, but now that it was stated he was sound again, and was coming back to the game, the records were overhauled, reminiscences were exchanged, memories raked up. Wasn't this the same Peter Dark who, six years before, had beaten off his own boot one of the finest teams Scotland had ever put into the field? Good egg, good egg again, seeing that Downside in the Second Round of the Cup had been drawn away against Heaton Athletic.

A little success will go a long way with the average football enthusiast. Although Heaton Athletic were a First Division club, and doing well it the League, principally on account of its rough-hewn defence, with its *nil desperandum* methods, the supporters of Downside — "the team that had risen from the dead" — saw no reason why they should be despondent.

The coming-back of Peter Dark lent support to this optimism; gave it solidity as it were. If he could show only a glimpse of his former skill, he would strengthen the Downside attack tremendously.

Perhaps it was the unconscious influence of McPhee. I have already tried to picture the Scot dreaming wonderful dreams, and seeing tantalising visions through the heavy reek of his pipe. Many obscure teams before Downside had achieved a momentary blaze of triumph during which they had won their First Round English Cup engagements. These other football suns had set as quickly as they had climbed the heavens. Downside might easily do the same.

With the superstition that every real lover of football unconsciously has in his heart, the Downside supporters felt that no further disaster could stay the progress of their team. The darkest hour had come before the dawn, which had been splendid and inspiriting. So it would continue. A man who could do what McPhee had done would not permit the team to slide. Men who would have mocked at such faith in their business life, swore by it when Downside's chances in the Cup were concerned.

Had not Second Division sides won the supreme honour before? Was it not notorious that clubs whose League records were too bad to be believed oftentimes went far in the English Cup Competition? Was not the resurrected Downside team playing captivating football?

The town of Downside was vibrant and alive with enthusiasm. The pent-up emotion of many years was now being given full vent. There is no such enthusiasm as the interest with which a team that shows a wonderful revival of form is followed. A club that is climbing out of despair to triumph — that is the team which breeds what superior people are apt to term football fanaticism.

So it was with Downside. Long before the day of the match, the newly-formed Supporters' Club had laboured and wrought to such an extent that it seemed likely there would be almost as much vocal support for the wearers of the scarlet jersey as for the black-and-white striped warriors of Heaton.

The distance between the two towns was but a beggarly eighty miles
– and what are eighty miles to the real football enthusiast? It was decided
that the team should travel to Heaton on the morning of the match –
"sleeping in a strange bed upsets some men," said Angus McPhee – and
that the 1,000 supporters of the Club who had chosen this, the best,
means of making the journey, should go with them.

The full flare of football enthusiasm is usually reserved for the semi-
final and final rounds of the Cup, but Downside, flushed with new-born
hope, were determined to make the best of the present occasion.

Outside the team itself, the most buoyant optimism prevailed; but in
the dressing-rooms and offices of Downside there was anxiety.

Although Walter Camp, the regular first team goalkeeper, was now fit
to resume, Giles, the team's best back, was sick.

CHAPTER XVI

GILES PLAYS IN CANVAS

Big football[6] at best is a lottery. So much depends on luck – or the lack of it. The most scrupulous care, for instance, cannot guard against accidents; and Giles' bruised ribs were the result of a pure accident. An ardent motor-cyclist, he had been out for a run on his machine on the Thursday prior to the match with Heaton, and a careless motor-car driver had caused him to make a violent swerve, as the result of which he had fallen heavily on his side.

The following morning, the back called McPhee in the dressing-room.

'Look at my right side,' he said.

The manager choked back an exclamation of dismay as he looked.

'I'm going to play on Saturday – mind that, Mr. McPhee,' cried the back in fierce defiance.

'Ye'll play if ye're fit – not unless!' McPhee was not used to having his authority defied, and he took the first opportunity of showing his resentment. But any private grievance he might have against the manner in which Giles had addressed him was forgotten in the bitter disappointment he felt at knowing that the best back he had on the Club books was in danger being incapacitated. Giles was a quiet, likeable player, who had been only too willing to learn. He had improved his game, and developed in a most surprising fashion during the past few weeks. Both in tackling and in his control of the ball he was fast becoming a master-back. Even now McPhee counted him likely to be one of the best defenders in the country next season, if he went on improving. He was relying on him to hold up the Heaton forwards on Saturday.

And now here he was showing ribs so badly bruised that playing football of any sort seemed an impossibility!

'Let me play, McPhee!' pleaded Giles. 'I didn't mean to be cocky just now – but I had set my mind on playing against the Athletic. You know that.'

---

[6] "Big Football" is the name that Horler often gave to the professional game.

'Aye, I ken that. I want ye to play. The question is: Can we get ye fit enough by 2.30 to-morrow afternoon? Pairsonally, I verra much doot it. I'll tell ye what to do; get into the taxi which ye'll find outside the gates in five minutes' time and go hame to bed. Ye have no' said onything aboot this to anyone else in the team, or oot o' it?' he queried.

'No, I didn't want to make a song about it.'

'I'm verra glad ye had that much sense, lad. If this had got aboot among the rest of the team, I should ha'e met nothin' but gloomy faces the day. The lads would ha'e lost hairt, and when the news had gone roond the toon, it would ha'e meant that the team's supporters might ha'e lost heart also. A bad thing, that, a mighty bad thing. Now, go hame quietly the noo, get to bed without sayin' a word, and presently, juist as soon as I can manage it, that is, I'll be along wi' the Club doctor. If ye can be made fit to play ye'll play. Ye ha'e shown sound common sense in not blabbin' so far; let me see that I can still depend on ye to keep your mouth shut.'

'I will that,' replied the right back, as he walked to the door.

McPhee watched him anxiously as he moved away. This was a bad blow, and his face showed it. But no good was ever done by bewailing one's lot. The thing to do was to try to get the wrong repaired. He accordingly went to the telephone and rang up the Club doctor.

Like everyone else having a close connection with the Downside F.C, Dr. David Blackley, the Club medical man, admitted to being enthusiastic. Debarred from playing himself by the handicap of a club foot, this young medico-man, a graduate of Edinburgh University, threw the whole force of his naturally buoyant nature into his job of keeping the Downside players Fit. It was a labour of love to him.

A brother Scot, he had taken to McPhee the first time he saw him. In their mutual love of football they met on common ground. They were a good combination; for while McPhee scorned fatigue in the matter of teaching the men under him how to improve their game, Dr. Blackley confessed that the most congenial and fascinating part of his large practice was to attend to his Downside "boys."

'I'll be round right away!' the doctor had told McPhee over the telephone; 'man, but this is bad news.'

He repeated this view an hour or so later after he had subjected the bruised ribs of the Downside back to a minute examination. 'There is nothing fractured or broken. and consequently the damage is not permanent – but as for your playing tomorrow, Giles, it is very doubtful. I'm sorry to have to say it.'

The back groaned. 'But isn't there any way out at all, doctor?' he pleaded; 'I tell you I'd as soon lose my left arm almost as miss the game! I don't know hardly how to put it but – well, I just wanted to show McPhee here how good he had made me… I want to do something for him in return, if you understand what I mean. Doctor, make me fit!'

'I wish I could, my lad!' answered the doctor, putting a hand on the player's shoulder. Giles was just a big schoolboy at that moment; in his simple, untutored way he had tried to express his surging feelings.

'Doctor,' said McPhee suddenly, and drew the other away from the bed. 'I'll juist ha'e a word wi' the doctor in private,' the manager added in explanation to Giles, who was looking at the two anxiously.

'Ye ken me well enough, I trust, doctor, not to think that I want to interfere with ye or your duties in ony way,' said McPhee. 'What I am goin' to say is juist by way of a wee suggestion, ye understan'?' The other nodded, and he continued: 'There was a seemilar case to this in France – when I was wi' the 5th Unbendables, ye ken. Our right-half had fallen into an old disused trench a night or so before we were to play the Borderers in the Final for the Brigade Cup. He *would* play, an' knowin' how keen the lad was (he was juist such another boy as Giles here), I patched him up somehow. And *he* had bruised ribs… Mind ye, it's only a suggestion; you can tak' it or leave it, juist as ye see fit.'

'What is it?' demanded the doctor, flicking his fingers impatiently.

'Well, I got some specially stiffened canvas from the Medical Corps and wrapped Nevis – that was the lad's name – in it. He looked top-heavy – but he played and lasted the game. If… ?

'I admit the risk,' he went on. 'And it's certainly true that the Athletic havena' the best of names. But it's their defence which isn't too particular. I dinna want to do onything which would cause this lad the slightest reesk of being pairmanently injured, but there's a lot at stake. I havena' a reserve back that I feel I could trust in this match.'

'Suppose we put it up to Giles, fairly and frankly?' rejoined the doctor, and with McPhee nodding his agreement, he turned towards the bed again.

'Giles,' he said, 'there is one chance of your being able to play to-morrow, but –'

'With all due respect to you, doctor, that's all I want to hear,' promptly replied the footballer; 'if it was left to me I'd go on if I could scarcely stand.'

'Of course, but that would be silly. Now, if I bandaged your ribs tightly just before the match, you would still feel a good deal of pain, no doubt, but I think you would be able to play – not as well as usual, perhaps, but still you could put up some sort of a decent show. But you would have to be careful in tackling. You might get a bad injury. Personally, as a medical man, I am not going to advise you to risk it –'

'That's all right, doctor!' said Giles, his face one huge smile; 'I'm going to play all right!' and he hopped out of bed, forgetting to wince with the pain that the action caused him.

'Ye get back to bed!' roared McPhee; 'didna I say ye had to rest?'

Downside was early abroad on the following morning. All through the previous night, parties of enthusiasts who could not or would not travel by the special train which was to leave the Central Station at 9.45, had left the town in charabancs, and other conveyances. Those doomed souls whose business or other ties kept them disconsolate in the town that day had to content themselves with thronging to the station to wish the departing team "good luck and the winning goal."

It was a memorable occasion. Long before the train was due to start, not only the railway platform but the entrance to the station was choked with people. As each player was noticed, he had a special cheer to himself. Football team managers are not usually subjects for personal demonstrations, but when the gaunt form of McPhee was seen limping towards them, the crowd gave a yell and there was a general surging forward in order to clap him on the back. So great became the press before the train could be reached, that not only the manager but the team were hemmed in.

'What are the chances, Mac?' called an eager voice.

McPhee, who with Dr. Blackley on the other side was principally concerned in safeguarding the bodily welfare of Giles, the player about whom he was so anxious, turned his grim face in the direction of his questioner, and replied: 'The chances are that if ye dinna gi'e way a good bit, ye folk, we shall never catch the train. And I'm telling ye, if ye hurt any one of my players...'

There was a general laugh at this, followed immediately by the foremost pressing backwards so that a passage could be cleared for the Downside team. There was another heave forward, however, when the chairman of the Downside Supporters' Club hove in sight proudly leading the team mascot, picturesquely attired in his uniform of Club colours.

At last everyone – including Neb – was safely aboard; the last ceremonies (including the fastening of a horseshoe to the engine) performed, and the long train steamed out amid the hurricane cheering of the crowd that was left behind.

'Many would say, no doubt, that that sort of thing,' said Dr. Blackley, who by much manoeuvring and the aid of a kindly hospital colleague had contrived to make the journey to Heaton, 'was supremely silly, but to my mind its rather wonderful. Have you ever considered, McPhee, what a tonic for humanity football can be? Let me tell you a recent experience.

The other week a man came to me. He said he was fed up with everything; had no interest in anything. Consequently he couldn't eat, sleep or think. Could I give him something? Could I suggest anything by which he could regain at least a slight desire to go on living? I am giving you his exact words.

'I sounded him and found that there was really nothing much wrong. Then I asked him if he had any hobby. Of course, I guessed he hadn't, because a man who had a decent hobby and took an intelligent interest in it, couldn't possibly have got into that deplorable condition.

' "No, I have never found any time for a hobby, doctor," he replied.

' "That's why you have come to me to-night,' I said. 'Now if I recommend a hobby which I think will do you a great deal of good, will you give it a trial?'

' "Certainly I will. I'll try anything! "Very well, then," ' I said; "go and see Downside play football next Saturday."

' "See who play what?" he cried.

'Really, I thought the fellow was going to jump out of his skin.

' "I mean it," I told him, 'and now I'm going to read you a little sermon, strictly from a doctor's point of view, of course. One of the chief reasons why men permit themselves to get into a run-down, morbid condition is because they never allow themselves time to cultivate a hobby. From a health point of view, I would go so far as to say that one of the greatest evils of to-day is that so few men and women have hobbies.

' "But watching football matches, doctor?" Really, I could have laughed; by the expression on the man's face I might have suggested shove-ha'penny or marbles.

' "Exactly! Football! You have asked me for advice, and give it to you. You shall have a bottle of medicine, but you can take my word for it, it won't do you nearly so much good as going to the football match next Saturday."

'Well, he went away, looking as though he suspected my sanity… but I noticed he's on this train to-day. And he's wearing his Downside favours as though he were mighty proud of them, as no doubt he is! There's a lesson in that, McPhee.'

'Aye, I ken that, doctor,' and McPhee fell to smoking furiously – he was thinking.

Having left one crowd behind: and brought another with them, Downside found a third awaiting .hem at Heaton Station. Directly the train pulled up at the platform this crowd thronged forward, a challenge in their eyes and mockery on their lips.

'Who killed poor Downside?' wailed a voice to the tune of "Cock Robin," and the answer came promptly:

' "I," said the Athletic,
Isn't it pathetic?'

This roused the fighting spirit of the staunch Downside henchmen, and verbal arrows, a few of them barbed, but most of them good-humoured, flew backwards and forwards. Amid this storm of badinage the Downside team descended from the train.

Progress was slow, however, for the stairs leading to the street were packed. Something had preceded the Downside team; it was the human interest with which all their present doings were invested.

Eventually a passage was won, and the team clambered up on a waiting charabanc. With McPhee sitting by the side of the driver, portentously solemn, the ponderous vehicle moved off, and the policemen on duty lost their worried look.

'Looks as if the town is all lit up, Peter,' observed Tommy Trott, with a grin.

It wasn't much of a reply, but it was sufficient for the inside-right. Trott guessed what was passing through his friend's mind; Dark was feeling like an actor coming back after a long absence to play a well-remembered and well-loved part. It was not a time for empty speech.

The fervour which gripped Heaton that day became more and more in evidence as the time drew near for the kick-off. The Athletic enclosure was supposed to hold not more than 50,000 (this record had been put up on the occasion of the League match with Hampton Villa, when the famous Birminster team and Heaton Athletic were running a neck-and-neck race for the First Division Championship six years before), but at 2.15 local judges gave as their opinion that the number had been exceeded.

With his usual good generalship, McPhee had left practically nothing to the last minute. The initial plan of campaign had been decided upon. This would be altered at half-time should the play demand an alteration. The men had been keyed up to tension-point, and the manager-trainer, with the help of Dr. Blackley, concentrated his energies on getting Giles fit for the fray.

'Jock's got a slight cold, so we are keeping his chest warm, boys,' remarked the doctor, as he wound the specially-prepared bandages round the back's chest.

The younger members of the team passed no comment; they were too preoccupied with their own condition to bother about anything else now that there were only a few minutes left before the start of the game, but Tommy Trott and Peter Dark, veterans in the art of war, exchanged significant glances. Seeing this, McPhee called them both over to the corner where the operation was being performed.

'Harry Thickett[7] stunt – only real this time, eh?' said the Downside captain. 'I wonder how much of that story was really true, Mac? Feel you'll last out, kid?' He turned to Giles.

'As long as my legs will hold me, Tommy,' grinned Giles cheerfully.

'That's the spirit, boy! That's the spirit of this team! Did you hear that, Peter?'

Dark, fully changed, nodded his head.

'Worth playing for, this team,' he commented laconically. Those who heard the words had occasion to recall them before the match was over.

Then, outside in the corridor, the referee's whistle shrilled, calling the teams to battle.

There can be real drama in football, and the 55,000 spectators of the Heaton Athletic v. Downside Cup-Tie saw it that day. It commenced with the kick-off and continued until the tired and exhausted players trooped into the dressing-looms some ninety-nine minutes later. Every one of those minutes had been packed with emotion.

The tense feelings of the crowd were reflected in the opening play, which was inclined to be wild. The men on either side made mistakes and committed blunders through nerves. The clamant cries of the rival supporters did not lessen the tension.

With a sympathetic insight into the cause, McPhee watched these early mistakes by his men. He had no fear about the team as a whole once this first attack of nervousness wore off, and the men got into their stride. He was chiefly concerned about Giles, and after Giles, Dark. Would the right back be able to stand the tremendous strain, and would Peter Dark justify the care he had taken with him? Would he, in other words, "come back?" It was as hard for a footballer as for a boxer. Yet he had faith in them both.

Within the first half-hour – during which, although the pace of the play was bewilderingly fast, nothing was scored – the manager's excusable uneasiness wore off. Giles did not throw himself into a tackle with the

---

[7] Harry Thickett was a sturdy right-back who played for Sheffield United. Not much would keep him off the field: injury, illness, bereavement. The story goes that he was injured before the 1899 Cup Final and that he had played swathed in 40 feet of bandages and fortified with whisky to deaden the pain. The story seems to have originated from a doctor specialising in football injuries in Manchester who Thickett had been referred to. A few days later he retracted the story saying he had spoken "in jest." Jest or a diplomatic retraction following ethical questions?

same joyous abandon as was customary with him, but in all other respects he was playing almost as well as ever. His partner, Gerrish, was better than usual, his covering tactics and position work being surprisingly good, so that the balance was kept even. It was a short journey from Jock Giles to Peter Dark – but what a vivid contrast in styles. One was Youth, eager-eyed, lusting in his strength in spite of his handicap, fretting with ambition. The other was Age, wise with experience, crafty with the gathered skill of years. Yet both were masters. Opening cautiously, the veteran inside-left had gained confidence as he found his once useless knee was so sound now that he could make any demand upon it, and soon the great crowd were staring at his witchery. The old £2,000 left foot had not lost its cunning. Time after time it swept the ball out in a perfect pass for young Finlay to take in his stride. Twice it had sent thunder-bolt balls flashing by the upright.

Yet it was Heaton that scored the first goal. Rallying to the insistent calls of the crowd, the home forwards swept down in a line. Just outside the penalty area the centre-forward slipped the ball to the inside-left. In rushing forward to dispossess the latter Giles, the Downside right back, was seen to halt suddenly, and put a hand to his right side. In that fatal moment of hesitancy the Heaton raider cut past him, diddled Gerrish as the latter came plunging across at too great a speed to retrieve himself should his first desperate tackle fail, dribbled on another three yards and then fired into the far top corner of the net well out of Camp's reach. It was a fine – a very fine – goal

No one among the 55,000 onlookers knew better than McPhee the tremendous moral value of that opening goal, but as he sprang up from his seat just inside the railings beneath the grand stand, his first thought was for Giles. Why had he put his hand to his side? From now until half-time he endured an agony of suspense, for he could not go on to the field unless the referee called him, and this the official did not do.

Once in the sanctuary of the dressing-room, Giles lifted a haggard face to the manager.

'It was my fault!' he said, dismally. 'I gave that goal away!'

'Ye did nothin' of the sort, lad… but I saw ye put your hand up to your side. Were your ribs hurting ye?'

'I don't know – I forget,' was the evasive reply. Giles, it was plain, was obsessed by one thought – that he had let his side down, and no misery was too great for him.

McPhee beckoned to the Club doctor. Blackley came running.

'I want the truth, my boy!' 'said the medical man sternly. 'How do you feel?'

'All right – honestly,' said the player, knowing what was in the doctor's mind.

Yet twenty minutes after the re-start the young Downside right back stopped suddenly again whilst running. This time he fell to the ground, and when his comrades ran towards him, he did not move. Then the referee blew his whistle, and to McPhee, who had come rushing across the churned turf, the official said five ominous words: 'He's fainted – take him off!'

It was a melancholy procession that filed into the visitors' dressing-room a few minutes later. Giles was still unconscious, and McPhee felt that he, and he alone, was to blame.

The doctor reassured him to the extent that no permanent harm was done to the player, and this somewhat eased his mind. Otherwise he would have been inconsolable.

'I let him play for his own guid, really,' he told Blackley. 'By playing he felt he could gi'e expression to what he felt – '

'And he'll be grateful to you for letting him have his wish. He fainted with the pain he must have suffered, but he'll be "round" very soon, and he won't suffer any ill-effects. I can assure you of that. Of course, he won't be able to go out again; and it's the team as a whole you've got to worry about now, Mac, not Giles.'

The feeling of worry was not confined to the visitors' dressing, room. It was rampant all round the enclosure wherever a Downside supporter stood. On the field of play the effect of the disaster to Giles showed in temporary faltering on the part of every member of the visiting team.

It was Peter Dark, the oldest player, but the latest recruit, who saved the situation. Dark was not a man for words. Ever since a boy he had always found it difficult to express himself except in moments of the greatest stress. But he was a man of deep feeling. He was full of gratitude to McPhee for bringing him back to football. He guessed what the Downside manager was thinking and dreading now that the visiting team was a player short[8] and a goal to the bad.

Downside must not lose!

Brilliantly as he had played in the first half, it was generally remarked that Peter Dark, the man whom no one thought would ever return to the game, was the outstanding figure on the field during the last twenty minutes of the game. The way he lasted was a revelation for a man of his age. He threw himself into the battle with the boundless energy of a youngster – but none or this energy was wasted. The old International was always scheming to some good purpose.

---

[8] Substitutions were not introduced until 1965/66 season.

Three times he seemed on the verge of scoring himself. As many times again he made openings for Gilligan, the centre-forward But this was not Gilligan's day.

The minutes seemed to fly round the watches that the desperately anxious Downside supporters pulled out of their pockets. The end – defeat – seemed inevitable; now there were only three more minutes to go. Still Downside played on, and while the referee was looking at his own watch, that veteran revived, Peter Dark, late of the Stars and England, came dribbling through the spent Heaton defenders in a last frantic effort.

But while it was frantic, Peter Dark kept his head – that wise old head which had planned so many football strategies in its time. Twice he feinted to pass, thus deceiving the home defenders so that he might make more ground.

'*Here*, Peter!' rose a strident yell.

Those who were near enough to the rails could see Peter Dark smile. He lifted his foot to shoot, drawing the goal-keeper (he had beaten everyone else in the Heaton rearguard) to his side of the goal. But in the same movement he flicked the ball to Tommy Trott, who had come rushing up like an express train.

The ball fell perfectly at the Downside captain's right foot. Without slackening in his stride, Trott hurled his whole weight at the ball. It scorched from his foot with such terrific force that the net at the back of the Heaton goalkeeper was torn up by its moorings.

For a single second the world seemed to stand still, and then the referee blew his whistle and pointed to the dressing-rooms.

Followed. Delirium…

The delirium was repeated on the following Wednesday. Downside, on their own midden, passed into the next round by two clear goals. The manner in which Peter Dark got both of these, it is safe to say, will pass into football fable.

Upon receiving the congratulations of McPhee, he made a rather significant reply.

'I owe you a lot,' he said, 'and that's something on account.'

CHAPTER XVII

THE HUNDRED THOUSAND GAME

After the spectacular victory over Heaton Athletic in the Second Round replay, McPhee's men seemed to take a delight (as one commentator pointed out) in confounding the critics. They passed from audacity to audacity – and each one was greater than the last. Thus, whilst in beating Heaton Athletic, even on their own around, they had upset the Book of Form, they further startled the sporting world in the next round by snatching a 3-1 win over those redoubtable Cup fighters, Middlesbridge, and finally convulsed everyone by emerging clear of both the Fourth and Semi-Final Rounds in which, after desperate struggles, they laid the hopes of Blackford Rovers and Wrington City in the mud of the playing pitches on which the games had been played. And both Blackford and Wrington City were not only First Division teams, but historic Cup fighters as well.

Anything can happen in football – especially in Cup-Ties – and it had happened now. The unquenchable fires of youth, hope and enthusiasm had carried Downside through to triumph when the chances seemed a hundred to one against them.

Even the indignantly surprised critics who before each game foretold that they were sure to be heavily defeated, were bound to admit Downside played good football. There was some reason for this, although the predominating impulse, the motive power, as it were, of the team was the flame of youth; but this splendid ardour was tempered, refined and strengthened by the more staple powers of men like John Hunter, Tommy Trott and Peter Dark.

Dark had repaid his debt to McPhee many times over. Not only had his knee completely stood the test, but he had come back to the game with the zest of a schoolboy. Football was his job, his trade, and Peter Dark believed in doing it well. Every time he turned out for Downside he did brilliantly. He scored in every Cup Tie, getting priceless goals with that cunning left foot of his against three of the best defences in the land.

McPatric, Scotland's captain and right back, played for Middlesbridge, and he made it his special duty to subjugate the Downside inside-left. In this he failed, for in getting the final Downside goal, the old Stars player left the Scottish International standing in the mud whilst he went on to ram home an express drive.

But Peter Dark was not the only shining light in the Finalists' front line. Trott, the captain, promised McPhee that he would play football from that time forward. Up to the time that the new Downside Club had emerged from the ashes of the old, Trott, a moody genius, had not troubled. What was the use? he would have said, had you questioned him.

The coming of Dark had been just the fillip he needed. If not so good a shot, Trott was almost as clever a dribbler and general ball-wizard as the former International and, in friendly rivalry with his old-time comrade, he never spared himself. In any case, he would have done this in fulfilment of his word to Angus McPhee, but the presence of Peter Dark in the team gave Trott an added stimulus.

The inclusion of the two amateurs, C. R. Aplin and John Hunter, also helped. Another of the absurd superstitions which exist in football is that professionals always resent playing alongside amateurs. A lot depends on the amateurs. There are good fellows amongst amateur footballers, and — others not so good. John Hunter had spent over fifteen years playing football alongside professionals. He liked them, and they liked him — no one could very well help liking this muscular Christian. Especially did he like the men who wore the Downside red jersey.

Shy and modest Aplin, the flying winger, waited for advances to be made to him by the professionals, but when these came (as they did after the first game with Heaton Athletic in the Second Round) he quickly responded. It did McPhee's heart good to watch the close friendship which existed between Tommy Trott and his young amateur partner. Aplin, only too pleased to pick up any wrinkles to improve his game, would spend hours practising schemes of play with the Downside captain.

The sporting pride of the town was wonderful to see; even the supporters of the high and mighty Rangers (who had dipped their colours in the First Round, much to the anguish of their boastful following), took a vicarious pride in the fact that the town was furnishing one of the teams for the Blue Ribbon event of the football year. What the matador is to Spain, the baseballer to America, the professional footballer is to England. He is the national sporting-gladiator — and the Downside players lived in a perpetual atmosphere of hero-worship. Had they not brought surpassing renown to their team and to the town? Nowadays even an ordinary ball practice could not be held without the banks being thronged with onlookers.

Prosperity had come with success. No longer were there any financial fears; wherever the Cup Finalists went, they drew enormous crowds, and at home their own enclosure was not nearly big enough to accommodate all the people who wanted to see the team of the year play. The popularity of the side was now something over which to marvel.

The Downside players gloried in the task which had been set them. The better the opposition, the better they played. Greatness in others had brought out greatness in themselves.

From goalkeeper to outside-left they one and all admitted that the quickening force which had always kept them up to concert pitch was the inspiration supplied to them by their team manager. He had been the Man Behind the Team.

He was the Man Behind the Team now as he fussed over the Downside players in the spacious dressing-room allotted to them on the wonderful new ground which had been got ready just in time for this soul-stirring spectacle. This was the first Final-Tie staged on the enclosure which the Football Association and erected in an endeavour to rival Scotland's classic ground, Hampden Park.[9]

McPhee looked drawn and worn. During the last four months he had worked early and late, doing many men's tasks, and although it was work near his heart, Nature was crying out for rest. But he could know not rest yet.

There were a hundred and one things for him to do. The nerves of most of the youngsters were twitching and throbbing. It was a case of soothing each with an appropriate word. Then Finlay, lean as a young greyhound, and as eager to let his flying feet go speeding, was complaining that his lunch, light as it had been, could not have agreed with him. Out flashed a small case from the trainer-manager's bag.

'Here! – this will put ye richt, lad,' said McPhee. He poured something out into a small glass, and after he had drank it off, the outside-left admitted that it had "done the trick." What was it? That is McPhee's secret.

So the work of preparation went on. A mere game of football! No, it was more than that, far more than that. This day would see the culmination of months of keenest preparation, would see bloom or wither the most cherished hopes. These men pulling on new scarlet jerseys and adjusting new black stockings with picturesque white tops, stood as national celebrities. Millions of men, women and boys (especially boys)

---

[9] McPhee was published in 1923, the same year that the first FA Cup Final was played at the newly constructed Wembley or Empire Stadium as it was first known.

could give details of their ages, weights, positions in the field, and for what clubs they previously played.

When a sport has taken such a hold as this upon a nation it cannot be dismissed as "a mere game of football." It must stand for something bigger. The Cup Final between Downside and Wildwood Town stood for the crowning glory of a season of wonderful football. It was an athletic contest which had sufficient attraction to draw over 100,000 spectators from all parts of the country. Millions more awaited the result with breathless excitement. Surely something more than a mere game of football...

The door of the Downside dressing-room was closely guarded. The manager had no wish to be churlish, but only those who had urgent business were admitted. In preparing his men for the most momentous battle of the year, McPhee had little time to waste on congratulatory addresses, idle queries and other verbal odds and ends. The congratulations could come later – after they had been earned.

But if the congratulations had to be deferred, the good wishes enthusiastic football followers from all over the country had sent to the team which had captured the public imagination poured in by telegraph. The telegrams wishing Downside luck had commenced to arrive soon after midday – there was a goodly pile of them awaiting the Downside players by the time they had arrived at their dressing-room. The flood did not cease until after the referee had poked his head round the door, and said in a tone that was good-humouredly serious: 'You are all going to be good boys to-day, I know.'

These telegrams had come from all sorts of people – from managements of clubs over which Downside had triumphed in the earlier rounds of the Cup, to private individuals. They were not all addressed to the Club itself, many were addressed to McPhee personally. One came from the Swifts, the club that had made him such a handsome offer before the Cup Ties came round.

These messages affected McPhee greatly. Aided by willing helpers and a set of circumstances which at first had looked to be hostile, but had really been fortunate – he had done something for the game, no doubt, but what had football done for him?

It had turned him into a celebrity. All the world knew now about Angus McPhee, the man who, one dark night, had drifted into Downside in a storm of rain and an unbelievable hat, and had proceeded to teach a team of hopeless failures how to play scientific football. The world had smiled when it first read of McPhee's blackboard strategies; but it stopped laughing when it read of Downside defeating teams in the Cup against which they did not appear to have the proverbial dog's chance.

Now that his team was actually in the Final, the world spent time in sending telegrams of congratulation to this wonder creator instead of laughing...

At length all were ready, and with Tommy Trott – the proudest man in England next to Angus McPhee – taking the lead, Downside filed out of the dressing-room.

Once out in the open the limelight was forced upon them. First, there was the Most Popular Personage, England's essentially sporting, and best Beloved Royal Young Man, to whom they were presented one by one. McPhee would have escaped from this glaring publicity, deep as was his admiration for Great Britain's worthiest ambassador, who had recently returned from a long tour overseas, but Tommy Trott would have none of it. When the Most Popular Personage remarked, as he warmly shook the Downside skipper's. hand, 'I congratulate you on captaining the most talked-of team of the season,' Trott immediately pointed to McPhee, who was standing by his side, and said: 'This is the man to congratulate, sir – McPhee's made the team what it is to-day!' The incident was not lost upon those members of the tremendous crowd who were near enough to witness it, and something occurred that was unprecedented in an English Cup Final.

Directly the Most Popular Personage had moved away, a brazen-voiced traveller from the wilds of Downside shouted at the top of his stupendous lungs: 'Three cheers for Angus McPhee!' For a single second it seemed that this startling innovation would be greeted with a death-like silence, but the next second the Downside contingent had taken up the challenge, and a wave of frantic cheering raced right round the enclosure.

McPhee walked to his trainer's seat, his rugged face flushed. In his wildest dreams there had never been anything so wonderful, so amazing as this. Had he not experienced it, he would have said that it was impossible to cram so much emotion into one day.

As he sat watching his team practising a brief preliminary "kick-in," while the referee strolled past, the brand new ball under his arm, a thrill of wonder passed through him. There were over 100,000 people grouped round the splash of green turf, criss-crossed with whitewash lines which was the stage for this tremendous football drama – and at least half of them wished him and his team well.

One hundred thousand men and women! To play before such an audience... to train men to play before such an audience. Ah!...

Two minutes later his men were showing the world the work he had done, and the crowd, tense and expectant, proclaimed that it was good.

CHAPTER XVIII

THE FINAL TRIUMPH

No less an authority than the wise and learned editor of the Athletic World (the Football Bible)[10] had said in summing up the chances: "Those who love a great game, classically played, should bud their heart's desire in this Final, which may easily become a classic, and pass into football history as a match worthy of the important occasion which has called it forth.'

Within five minutes of the start, it seemed probable that the prediction of the greatest writer and critic the game has ever produced would be realised. The early thrusts and parries gave promise of tremendous things.

The Wildwood Town team was a curious blend of ultra-classicism and rough-hewn resolution. The forwards worked the miracles, and the defence trampled on the opposition. This combination of brain and brawn had been effective throughout the season.

Wildwood were confident that these tactics would prove equally effective in the Final. Alter all, Downside was still only half-way up the Second Division table, while they (the Town) were fourth from the leaders in the First Division chart.

But the forwards who had made so many other defences look foolish, found themselves held. Playing right up on top of their opponents, John Hunter, Dixon and Harrigan policed these cunning schemers in the old-gold and maroon jerseys so despotically, that many a promising movement was strangled at birth. In doing this, the Downside halves were steadfastly carrying out the first of the tactics laid down by their trainer.

____

[10] This is a clear reference to James Catton who edited the *Athletic News*, the leading nationally distributed newspaper dedicated to Sport, and in particular football in the late 1800 to the 1920s. Think John Motson and Kenneth Wostenholme rolled into one and you get an idea of Catton's stature in the game.

'Smother their forwards at the start – it will help to break their hearts; then our own lads can get a chance.'

So the Downside half-backs had watched ceaselessly, and tackled the instant the opposing front line touched the ball. Grimly tenacious, they were giving the Town raiders no rope.

But the Downside team had not the monopoly of football brains on this historic day. For fifteen minutes the famous forward line, which had been expected to charm and wheedle its way by sheer magic through the Downside defence, was checked. restrained, frustrated. The crowd, gripped by such masterly tactics, reserved a special place in their affectionate admiration for John Hunter, parson and sportsman, whose keen and incisive tackling was a joy to anyone with red blood racing through his veins.

At the end of the first quarter of an hour, however, a change came over the scene. The Wildwood backs advanced and, instead of placing discreetly to their forwards, as they had done previously, they booted the ball with lusty vigour and fierce abandon. Their heavy guns extended their range. This change in the play led to Giles and Gerrish being hustled.

But they held their fort. These two youngsters had both shown before that they had the right temperament for big events. Now that the biggest occasion of all had arrived, they proved incontestably the men for the job. Giles, who had fully recovered from his mishap, was the better of the pair, his intuition of the run of the play being admirable, and his partner was little behind him.

From now on it was a battle of wits as well as of feet and limbs So swiftly changing was the game that it became kaleidoscopic in its infinite variety. Men with grey frosting in their hair said openly they had not seen football of this quality for over ten years. For once a Cup Final was being seen that was worthy of the occasion.

The pace was bewildering. Fierce excitement possessed players and onlookers alike. Craft was allied to speed, and the standard of the football was almost incredibly high for a Cup Final.

Nothing was sacrificed for mere speed. Thrust and parry, parry and thrust – with nothing but tutored toes and a football for weapons. Yet one hundred thousand spectators were held fascinated.

Such a standard could not last; it was impossible. Something would be bound to give. It was the Wildwood defence which gave. Supremely confident at first, the Town meant to mesmerise their opponents during the first quarter of an hour. When they found they could not break through the impregnable half-back line that hedged their forwards about, they changed their tactics. They still played supremely clever football – they could not help doing that – but they cut out over-elaboration and forced the pace. Here again, however, they found that they were checkmated, and that they had met their match.

If anything, this disturbing fact made them play above themselves rather than otherwise. The result was seen in a wonderful thirty minutes of scintillating football which recalled to so many old-stagers present the undying deeds of some of the Old Masters of the game.

Thirty minutes' brilliance – and then something cracked. All this while Downside had never tired. They were playing like a machine, perfectly managed and flawless in every part. A common spirit was animating every member of the side. From this they derived a harmonious strength that kept their skilful fellowship intact.

At the end of the thirty minutes, even the iron men in the Wildwood defence commenced to waver. One can beat a human being, but not a machine. No matter how many times they were frustrated and toiled, the five players composing the Downside front line kept speeding back, apparently unruffled, obviously unfatigued.

It was good to see. Peter Dark and Tommy Trott were as cunning as monkeys, and as agile. Many of their schemes were broken on the rock-like Wildwood defence, but when this weakened at last (as both knew it would be bound to weaken in course of time) they accomplished their end.

By the finest concerted play they had yet shown, they left both Wildwood backs gasping. Trott was left with the ball. It looked at first as though it might be going over the line, but with a quick swing of his right, he lifted it into the goal-mouth, and here Gilligan, the Downside centre-forward, slammed it past Bryant, the Wildwood goalkeeper first, and jumped high into the air in ecstasy immediately afterwards.

First blood to Downside! – and none could say they had not deserved it.

But Wildwood were not beaten. Like Downside, they had tradition upon which to draw. The memories of the past great glories of the club sustained and upheld the present players in this moment of bitterness, when all the world seemed awry. The first goal in a Final Tie is of incalculable worth; its moral value is immeasurable. But Wildwood Town, shaking itself like an enraged lion, gritted its teeth and carried on.

Dixon, the Downside centre-half, over-confident, perhaps, at the success of the man immediately in front of him, was just a trifle late. Wilcox, the Wildwood sharpshooter, stormed a passage which caused the still-jubilant cries of the Downside supporters to die in their throats. Swift as a hare Wilcox ran, and before Giles or Gerrish could close on him, he had flashed a high, swift shot straight for that angle which the upright of the goal makes with the cross-bar.

The ball was nothing but a streak of brown flame – this shot might have beaten any man – but Walter Camp sprang at it like a cat, punched it clear, caught it again as it descended, swerved as Wilcox, lusting for the equalising goal, sprang at him, slipped in the treacherous slime of the goal-mouth, and finally punted clear while a hundred thousand people stood on tiptoe and cheered him as though he were a god.

This was splendid! Glorious for Downside! The thrilling act breathed defiance. It said as plainly as words: "What is the use, you wild men from Wildwood?" There was an audacity about it that was almost insulting. Few goalkeepers have the grand manner, but Walter Camp, who stood in Downside's goal-mouth, was one of them. There was a suggestion of Doig, a reminiscence of L. R. Roose in his play.[11] Much he had possessed before; but McPhee had added to his store. He had rounded off the rough corners. Camp was now superb.

Breathing more freely now that this spirited sally of the opposition had been beaten off, Downside came again. This time Aplin led the raid. It was a splendid run, and the young amateur was in the act of completing it by centring when the Wildwood left back charged him heavily. The outside-right, unable to prepare himself for the shock, collapsed with a groan…

McPhee, aroused from the trance into which the excellence of the play had sent him, scuttled across the playing pitch. One glance was enough – Charles Aplin would play no more that day. Even before the ambulance men, whom the referee had summoned after looking appraisingly at the prostrate player, McPhee knew that Aplin, in falling so heavily, had fractured at least one rib.

'It wasn't intentional – I'm a heavy fellow, and I let him have all I got – but it wasn't a foul.' The Wildwood left back spoke straightly, if contritely.

'I know that – it's all in the game,' responded McPhee, and followed behind the ambulance men carrying their melancholy burden.

It had been an accident all right – but it might mean that the English Cup would go to Wildwood, and not Downside.

You cannot take away any essential part of a smooth-working machine without it suffering. Ten men cannot do the work of eleven. John Hunter tried to be forward and half-back in one, but the extra toil told heavily on him, so that Speedie, the Wildwood outside-left, five

---

[11] John Doig was Sunderland's Scottish international keeper in the 1890s when they were amongst the best in the country. The amateur keeper Leigh Richmond Roose was an unconventional/eccentric Welsh international renowned for his 40 clean sheets in his 147 appearances for Stoke; he played for other clubs including Sunderland and Aberystwyth Town; he was killed in the Battle of the Somme in 1916.

minutes after the accident, ran clear away from the gaoler who had thus
far shadowed him so effectively.

He made the most of this unexpected freedom, rushing past Giles
like a bird in flight. And he finished as well as he had begun, lobbing
across such an ideal ball that all the lengthy Wilcox had to do was to nod
it into the net out of the reach of Camp, whose fingers touched the ball,
but could not hold it.

Thus equality – and Downside with only ten men.

Shortly after the half-time whistle shrilled, and the Downside team
trooped into the dressing-room to find Aplin pleading eloquently with the
Club doctor to allow him to go on to the field in the second half.

'Certainly not! It would be madness! I have already told you that one
of your ribs on the left side is badly fractured. Why, you could scarcely
run, let alone stand being hustled. A heavy charge might… well, I won't
take any responsibility it you don't listen to what I say! Good Lord, man!
It hurts me like hell to have to tell you – but there it is. Things couldn't be
much worse, could they?' Blackley added, turning to McPhee.

The latter snatched the bottle of smelling-salts which the doctor had
been holding from Blackley's hand and crossed to the incapacitated right
winger. Aplin was crying like a child.

'I've lost the Cup for you, McPhee,' he said, hysterically; but McPhee
patted him on the back.

'My bad luck is nothing to yours, my boy. Have a sniff o' this – it'll
pull ye together.' A moment later the ambulance men came to take the
victim of the accident away to the hospital.

So to the second half – and further disaster. Five minutes after the
resumption John Hunter, the comrade of the absent Aplin, rose limping
from a tackle, and made a wry face at McPhee, who again came running
forward.

'Something's gone – can't run. But I'm going to stick it. May be
better presently.' He waved the trainer away, and hobbled ahead; but it
was plain he was in physical torture.

He went to outside-right – the only position he could take up; and
now it was Tommy Trott's turn to fetch and carry, to be half-back and
forward in one. Yet when he had the ball he could pass it only to his left,
for on his right was a hobbling cripple. The betting, had there been any[12],
would have slumped to at least three to one in Wildwood's favour. Eleven
sound men were against ten – and one of them a cripple!'

'Come on the nine men!'

---

[12] The only legal form of sports gambling was on-course betting on horses, until the
football pools were introduced as a "game of skill" in 1923 and then bets allowed at dog-
tracks in 1926.

The strident rally to arms rang out like a trumpet-call. And the nine men came on. But they could not prevail. They might have done it, if only John Hunter could have got to the ball that had rebounded from the left upright in time. But the Downside man was lame – pitiably so – and the chance was lost. The ball went weakly over the line – outside.

As the Downside men moved back to take up their position for the goal-kick, Trott was seen to wave his hands and talk excitedly. The crowd became agog. With one man off and another a hopeless cripple, what plan of strategy was the Downside skipper instructing his men to follow? Even the vaunted genius of the man whose orders he was carrying out could not avail, it seemed, now that the odds were so heavily against his team.

'Come on the nine men!' shouted the Downside challenger again.

But apparently Downside had shot its bolt. The flood of misfortunes which had come to them had sapped their strength, and broken their spirit. On the principle that half a loaf was better than no bread, they seemed content with the possibility of a draw. They concentrated on defence, and let attack alone. Why attack with three men?

From the strategical point of view, it was sound politics, no doubt. Why attempt the impossible with so much at stake? If the present match were left drawn, there would be a replay, and on the second occasion luck might be kinder to them.

The play became dour and grim. It had lost the showy brilliance of the first half. It had taken on a new aspect. Could the nine men and a cripple keep the opposition at bay? That was the question. It was only nine men now, for, seeing no doubt what pain he was in, the crowd noted McPhee, the Downside manager and trainer, went to the touch-line and had a few earnest words with John Hunter, the crippled hall-back. Hunter immediately left the field.

Sympathy is ever with the bottom dog – and Downside was indubitably the bottom dog on this occasion. Although the great crowd felt sorry that the game which had opened so well should have been robbed of its brilliance, it did not stop cheering. After all, the play now had a new, if different, piquancy.

Could Downside hold out? Desperate as were the attacks which Wildwood launched, they were still being beaten off. Both the inside-left and inside-right had fallen back to the assistance of their comrades in the Downside defence, and only Gilligan, the centre-forward, and Finlay, the outside-left, endeavoured to keep their positions in the once scintillating forward line. The sight brought a lump into Downside throats.

The Wildwood men had been revived by champagne at the interval, and they attacked like hungry wolves. Yet the Downside defence continued to be worthy of an epic. If the spectators could no longer see how Downside trained its forwards, it could see how it developed its backs. Giles and Gerrish were super-men; they guarded their goal as though it held their personal honour; as, indeed, it did.

Faster and faster the battle raged; the Wildwood forwards worked themselves into fiercer frenzies as the minutes went by. To be held up like this… it was intolerable. So intolerable did Wilcox, the burly centre-forward, find the conditions after Giles, tingling with life, had dived and taken the ball audaciously from off his very toes, that he forgot himself and the great occasion. Glaring and glowering, he essayed a furtive kick at the youngster's shin. For this Giles knocked him purling the next time the two met; a perfectly fair shoulder charge. The referee scoffed at the Wildwood clamourings for a foul.

'Play the game!' he said, and waved them off.

Twenty minutes, ten minutes to go! Still the Downside defence held out. Then, quite visibly, Wildwood tired. Well trained as they had been, human flesh and blood could not keep up the terrific pace at which this second half had been played.

The snap now went out of their limbs, the fire out of their play. The danger to Downside was past. The foe's guns were spiked. The game must end in a draw. Tens of thousands among those who watched would have bet money on it.

Eight minutes to go, and Tommy Trott, the Downside skipper, clapped his hands. Like an army battalion advancing to the attack, the Downside team moved up the field. Even Walter Camp slipped a pace out of the goal he had guarded so well. Down on the trainer's bench beneath the towering grand-stand, black with people, McPhee craned forward, his eyes alight…

Right from the throw in, Wildwood sensed the danger. They were tired men. Their opponents had worn them down and out. They, too, should have felt the tremendous strain. Most of them did, no doubt; yet Peter Dark came weaving a path through the jaded ranks of Wildwood. He pushed the ball forward to Gilligan. The centre swooped on it sideways, and burst away.

Now the crowd could see! With a purposeful cunning, Downside had contented themselves with defence until the right moment. Then they had faced about to rend the enemy.

The strategy – masterly in its very simplicity – was plain. Gilligan, the mooning centre-forward, brooding alone in the middle of the playing pitch doing nothing, had been kept in reserve. He had never fallen back to help the defence. When the ball had come to him, he had merely booted it away, never attempting to dribble. But now Downside were staking their all on him – on his young strength which, by obvious orders, had been so carefully husbanded. This sudden meteoric dash of his was the most dramatic stroke of the whole game.

Over 100,000 people, tense, and braced for either overwhelming joy or the most poignant sorrow, held their breath. Gilligan sped on, a human hurricane in action. The move had turned the whole tide of the game. A dour defence had been changed into an audacious attack. It was so unexpected that the Wildwood backs started too late to overtake this greyhound. Unless Gilligan tripped, or fell over the ball which was so snug at his toes, they could only pound heavily and desperately at his heels.

That was the psychological side of this strategy which had been planned. McPhee had sought to turn the misfortune that had crippled his team to his own uses. He wished to create the impression of a forlorn team, a mere remnant of a fighting side. That was why he had withdrawn John Hunter from the field. By doing this he made the forward line look pitiable – from a practical attacking point of view almost entirely negligible.

It was to strengthen this impression that Trott had carried out his manager's instructions by ordering the whole team to act on the defensive.

Then that sudden burst of flame...

Gilligan was all fire, but he kept his head level. His brain was clear, and that right foot with which he would presently shoot was true. He knew that everything depended on him. Great as would be his personal glory if he succeeded, greater still would be the shame and ignominy should he fail.

He could see Bryant, nervous as a cat, prancing in his goal. He saw the goalkeeper suddenly leap outwards at him. This was his testing time, and he knew it. The slightest hesitation now, and he would be lost.

The tremendous responsibility which was his frightened him. He lunged forward and smote the ball. It went hissing from his foot, swift and true for the corner of the goal.

Like an acrobat, the Wildwood goalkeeper flung himself sideways. His outstretched fingers touched the ball, but he could only throw it weakly from him...

The craning crowd saw a form in a scarlet jersey bound forward as though he had been a piece of rubber. It was Tommy Trott who, with every ounce of strength left in him, called upon his tired muscles and aching nerves to make this last tremendous effort. The Downside captain flicked the ball deftly over the prostrate body of the goalkeeper and, in the very act of reeling from the heavy charge of the Wildwood left back, sent it spinning into the empty net.

The heavens seemed to split and the earth to shake, so deafening was the uproar as the ball crossed the line.

There were three whole minutes left for play. But who cared? Crowd and players alike were shaken with the force of the dynamic stroke which had won the English Cup for Downside.

CHAPTER XIX

ANGUS McPHEE – BEST MAN

The Town Hall was by far the biggest building in Downside, but even that was found to be much too small. The surging crowds that still demanded admittance beat about the shut doors in dense waves. While they swayed this way and that, they called a name:

'*McPhee!*' they cried.

Inside a tall, gaunt man, twirling awkwardly in his right hand a really dreadful hat, stood on the platform while the Mayor of the town spoke honeyed words.

To McPhee the Mayor's voice seemed to drone from a great distance, with now and then strange crescendo effects. He caught a few words. Then the voice would be winded away, until the next crescendo brought back to him another waft of words... 'proud to be here to-night... brought home the English Cup... our heart-felt thanks... due principally to the efforts of one man... started a public testimonial... I like a bit of sentiment... my capacity as chief magistrate... Mr. Angus McPhee.'

Then came a great gust of sound, hats and handkerchiefs waved, people clambered on seats and shouted. McPhee felt giddy with the continuous movement. He blinked his eyes rapidly. There seemed to be grit beneath the lids. It must be the dust due to the stamping. It –

'Giles, our right back,' the Mayor was speaking again. 'Picked up the ball... became his own property... well-known tradition... signed by each player... glass case on gold pedestal... a gift from Downside... one and only McPhee.'

What happened after that McPhee never knew. The dust became intolerable. It made his eyes stream. Somebody hit him on the back and he dropped his hat. A moment later he was trying to pick up the Mayor's boot...

'Some more callers, Mister McPhee,' announced Mrs. Biggin late that night, in a tone of uncompromising disapproval.

The next second two people precipitated themselves tempestuously into the room. The first was "Happy" Howard, his eyeglasses askew, his necktie twisted, and his hair rumpled. He held by the hand a radiant, but slightly dishevelled Nancy Spurgeon.

'Got a job of work for you, Mac!' cried Howard. 'Nancy and I are going to get married, and we want you to be best man!'

'Why?' asked McPhee, staring at Nancy with horror-stricken eyes.

'Because we've got you to thank for it! That's why! Old Sam's (excuse me, Nancy) in such a good humour about Downside winning the Cup that he didn't raise the least objection when I asked him. I've got a better job, and I've made enough money out of Downside football to buy some real furniture! It's all through you, old son! That's why we want you to be best man. In fact, you've *got* to be best man. Nancy insists. We're all footballers – in one way or another.'

'Mr. McPhee,' said Nancy roguishly, 'you *must* be there at the kick-off...'

'Well, lassie,' replied Angus McPhee, 'yon's a new game to me, but I'll promise ye I'll look up the book o' rules! Ye're a fine team, an' I wouldna' do onythin' to spoil your combination; but I'm sair afraid o' weddin's,' and he shook his head with a mournfulness that his eyes belied.

THE END

Dear Reader

If you thought this book was at least mildly entertaining, it would be really appreciated if you could do a quick review on Amazon, Goodreads or other online sites you use. Just a word or two would be great. 1889 Books is a small-scale undertaking so word of mouth is vital to letting readers know about it.

You can sign up for news and offers at www.1889books.co.uk, such as a free e-book of my first novel *The Evergreen in Red and White* set in Sheffield in 1897/98, based on the true story of Rabbi Howell, the first Romani international footballer.

I have published several other great books with a football theme including another Sydner Horler classic, *On the Ball,* and the superb *Ghosts of Inchmery Road* by Mat Guy. Please see: www.1889books.co.uk